I0819978

THE VIOLENCE OF REASON

PETE PLANISEK

Book by Pete Planisek

Cover design by Pete Planisek, Elizabeth Nordquest, and Scott Coons
Photo of stave church by Kevin and Debbie Skarsten

The Violence of Reason/Pete Planisek

ISBN: 978-0-9850982-7-8 (ebook)
ISBN: 978-0-9850982-8-5 (print)

Enceladus Literary is a registered trademark.

Ebook released in the United States of America

Published by Enceladus Literary LLC
Columbus, OH

www.enceladusliterary.com

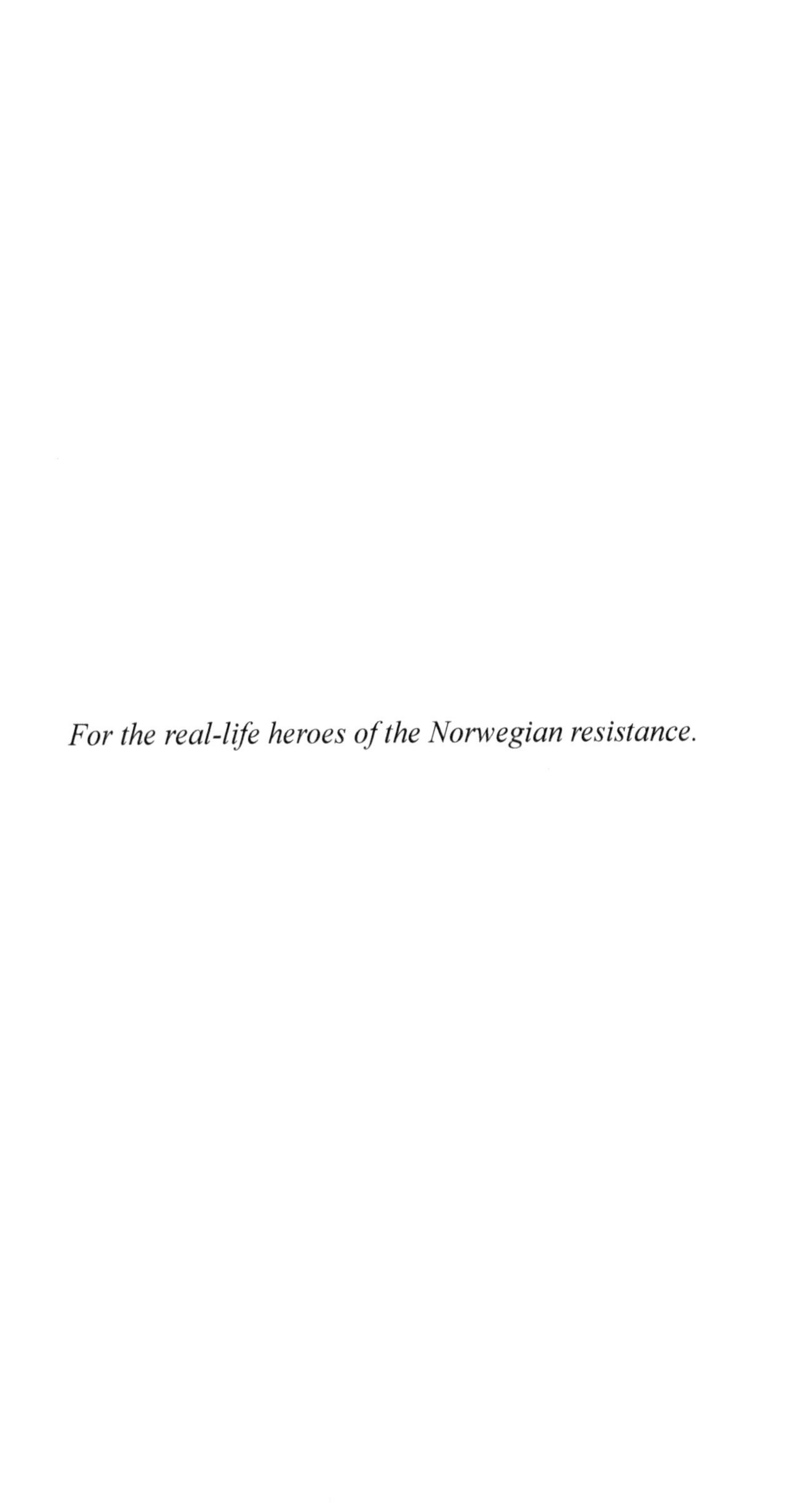

For the real-life heroes of the Norwegian resistance.

CHAPTERS

CHAPTER ONE

A FATEFUL VISIT

Norill's back involuntarily straightened as the front door swung open moments after the hasty knock that preceded the action.

"*Guten morgan*, may we come in?" one of the Nazi soldiers politely inquired.

The three had already begun to file inside so there was little point in protesting. Norill wordlessly retreated to the nearest stool lest one of them try to sit next to her on the sofa. She would have offered her companion a look of wariness but to do so would have been pointless. Besides, Vinni could probably already sense her discomfort, even if she couldn't see it.

"And what can I do for you gentlemen today?" Vinni smoothly requested as she stood, betraying no fear of the armed, enemy soldiers now standing in her home.

"We heard you playing just now. *Mein freund*, here *ist* interested in lessons, like your sign says," one of the men stated as they all carefully studied the small front room.

"Piano I assume," Vinni warmly smiled, gesturing to the instrument behind her back.

Norill shifted uncomfortably and attempted to busy herself so as not to make eye contact with any of the soldiers, especially the one supposedly interested in lessons. This, unfortunately, was not her first encounter with him. Ever since the Nazis unwelcome arrival in Norway and the town's occupation, it had become very clear to Norill that he took an active interest in her activities. They had never spoken directly, but it felt like he was always somehow present, ominously watching her, just as he did now. She was both infuriated and terrified that he stood in the same room with her.

"Of course, I took lessons as a boy and I'd like to take up playing again," the soldier asserted.

"Certainly. Norill is one of my more advanced students and volunteers as my assistant sometimes when she is free,"

Vinni explained, aware of where the Nazi speaker's attention was currently focused.

Norill nodded to the soldiers but did not meet their eyes. A stillness filled the room for an unnatural measure.

"Yes, of course," her unwanted solicitor finally replied as he returned his full attention to Vinni.

"A most charming companion," another added, seeing Norill's uneasiness.

"Please describe your precise role here," the eldest soldier said, his face passive but his voice leaving no doubt that the "please" was perfunctory. This was an order, not a request.

Norill shuffled some nearby papers, hoping they did not take note of the paperclip on the lapel of her coat. This symbol of Norwegian unity was common enough, but under the soldiers' gaze she still felt abundantly aware of its presence.

"My brother is also blind, so I learned braille as a child. I translate sheet music to and from braille for Mrs. Naess and help her with lessons and housework as needed," Norill calmly said as she succinctly met each of their eyes. "I also work at the local bookshop."

"A blind piano teacher," the eldest soldier remarked as his smug visage regarded Vinni Naess with incredulity.

The older woman resumed the bench, turned back to her piano, and began to play; her fingers tracing the braille sheet music. It was a short but impressive display of her extensive talent. The performance elicited a flicker of a smile from the two younger men but a look of reproach from the other.

"Chopin was French," the eldest soldier scolded with an air of annoyance. "Surely even an undesirable like you must know of our cultural edicts."

Vinni brushed aside the insult with a warm smile.

"Actually, he was Polish by birth, but I suppose you want something by a Germanic composer," Vinni noted as she switched effortlessly to Bach.

"It is more fitting given Vidkun Quisling's[1] cultural decrees for loyal Norwegians," the eldest soldier commented by way of both warning and agreement.

For a few peaceful minutes, they all simply listened to Vinni as she played.

Norill weighed her options. Undoubtedly, Vinni had chosen this piece to allow her time to gather her thoughts. Should she claim that no lesson times were currently available? They might come back more often then. At least if she scheduled a day and time they would know exactly when the Nazi would return. Still, allowing him here was dangerous - very dangerous.

She sighed inwardly. Perhaps it was fate that brought them here for either path she chose in the moments to come presented danger to them all.

This time the soldiers all civilly clapped as Vinni finished playing. The heavier-set woman gave a curt nod of appreciation before turning to Norill, who remained stoic. Vinni was the leader here. She must be the one to decide. The older woman paused before returning her attention fully to the assembled Nazi soldiers.

Will you be paying in krones or Reichsmarks?"

Vinni negotiated a reasonable price for her services and instructed Norill to schedule the Nazi soldier, named Gerntz, for 4:00 P.M. on Tuesdays. Their business concluded, the Nazis left and both women breathed sighs of relief into the tense quiet that followed.

"Are you crazy," Norill finally asked. "We can't have that officer coming here."

Vinni sat back heavily against the keyboard and shook her head.

---

1 Norwegian politician and Nazi collaborator during German occupation of Norway during World War II.

"It's the Web of Wyrd[2]. Our fate was fixed the instant they set foot inside this house. Send them away from a blind woman offering piano lessons empty-handed and the questions will begin. Questions we can't have them asking. Not unless you want them discovering what we're truly doing. At least this way we can watch them."

"And he can watch us … watch me," Norill bitterly countered.

"Do you think this Gerntz suspects you of being resistance?" Vinni demanded.

Norill reflected on this question as she hunched forward.

"I can't be sure. Maybe. His friends certainly aren't the trusting type. No, his interest in me is more … personal. I've seen him watching me for several weeks now. Not following me but …," her left fingers clasped her right shoulder in consternation. She knew what this man wanted.

Norill knew other girls, some of whom were once friends, who had begun romances with these occupying soldiers. Once they were fully trusted by the Nazis, they were granted extra rations, privileges, taken to expensive parties, and loathed by their fellow Norwegians for they had forsaken all that their loyal countrymen and their Allies fought and died for. Traitors to all for their own creature comforts. She would not become that.

Norill would never be that.

Norway may be occupied, but her spirit remained indomitable and that was something the Nazis and their puppet government under Vidkun Quisling could not stand. They wanted to insidiously reshape all of Norway into a state filled with fascist collaborators. It was seeing this attempt day in and day out that inspired Norill to channel her anger and efforts into supporting the *Milorg*, the Norwegian resistance,

---

2 Legend of web that was woven by the Nornir, Norse mythological fates, that created the fate of all beings.

even though exposure with such activities would mean either imprisonment or more likely execution.

Vinni had joined the resistance not long after the government attempted to force teachers like her to embrace a pro-fascist curriculum for their students. So far, the government's efforts were failing, but no one knew what the ultimate outcome would be.

"We can use that interest of his," Vinni said, leaning towards her companion.

"What?" Norill recoiled at the idea. "He'll kill me if he finds out we're using him."

She stood and began to pace. This was unfair. Norill wanted this man, and all like him, out of her life, not closer.

Vinni remained quiet as she considered the full reality of what she was contemplating. Was she ready to put Norill into such danger?

Although the young woman was basically a daughter to her, the opportunity to gain intelligence and make a real difference in the war effort was undeniable. The risk, though difficult, acceptable.

"I don't propose this lightly, Norill. But, if he is as persistent as you think, we cannot afford for him not to think his advances aren't working. Imagine the intelligence we could gather from him. Your efforts might even save countless lives …"

"No," Norill flatly declared, shaking a blonde curl away from her eye as she stomped her foot before nervously crossing the room to pull aside the curtain to check the street outside. Only empty windows from the closely packed buildings and a vacant cobblestone road greeted her gaze.

"Looks like we're clear," she said, inwardly berating herself for such a reckless outburst. "Hopefully, Haktor got a chance to finish transmitting," Norill added, wishing for nothing more than a change in the subject between them.

The older woman nodded, aware that to press further would gain her very little with Norill. Still she could not resist offering one final plea.

"Well, just consider what I said about Gerntz."

Vinni played a short sequence of notes—the signal to the radio operator hidden in the attic that the downstairs was safe. They heard the normal muffled sounds as Haktor extracted himself from the cramped, secret transmission room in the attic and made his way downstairs.

"Tell me what happened," the bald man with the untamed beard demanded immediately upon his appearance on the staircase.

"We had a customer," Vinni evenly informed him as Norill helped her up from the piano bench and to a more welcoming chair. "A Nazi with a taste for piano lessons, among other things, and a few of his friends. They've gone but he'll be back Tuesday afternoon for a lesson."

Haktor, who rented a spare room from Vinni, was a fisherman by trade, and Norill noticed whenever he received bad news, the weathered lines of his face seemed to grow more pronounced. In fact, his years spent on the water had seasoned his face so unnaturally, it was seemingly impossible to guess his exact age. Still, that did not discourage Norill and Vinni from keeping an unofficial bet as to what it might be. Haktor was completely ignorant of their little game but, perhaps, one day, they would learn whose guess was closest.

"Are we compromised?" Haktor questioned, ready to clamber upstairs to destroy the radio equipment.

"Doubtful. It seems my future student is enamored with my current protégé, and that is what brought him here," Vinni explained.

"Then we need to get her out of here," Haktor decided, absently stroking his uncultivated beard. "Don't give him a reason to return. Let it be known that you fired her or that there was a falling out."

"Suddenly. So soon after their visit?" the old woman challenged. "No. That's far too suspicious behavior to be considered coincidence. A week or two and we may be able to send Norill away to a safe house under the pretense of visiting family without arousing questions, but I fear that's the best we can do," Vinni let her hands fall into her lap.

Haktor was noticeably displeased but he said no more.

"Were you able to finish securing today's signals?" Norill inquired.

"Aye."

Troubled, Haktor hesitated before handing the messages over so Norill could begin to encode each into sheet music, which she would then safely convey to the resistance newspaper for decoding and printing.

She reviewed the messages.

"Oh God, not again. The Germans have eradicated another resistance cell," she told Vinni.

The old woman's mouth drew open in horror before she closed her eyes.

"Slaughtered. That's the fourth one in as many weeks," Haktor reminded them. "The only way they can be having this kind of success …"

"Is if they've inserted a double agent," Vinni finished as she reopened her eyes.

"That's what did a lot of cells in during the early days of the resistance," Haktor bitterly shared as he turned and looked meaningfully at his young compatriot. "We thought we'd solved that problem."

Norill turned away, lost in reverie as she wondered which of her friends could now be on the run, imprisoned, or dead.

No one spoke.

"Hopefully, someone survived this time," Vinni finally said. "It may be the only way we'll ever be able to discover and root out this evil."

"If this continues, this entire section of Norway could see the resistance crumble," Haktor darkly mused.

"A bit bold but our operations are definitely being impacted. I wonder how long the British will continue to trust us with intel if this goes unchecked?" Vinni wondered aloud.

The three shifted with tension but there was nothing left to say.

"I'll be in the signal room encoding this if you need me," Norill decisively announced before quietly ascending to the dark, dimly lit confines of the attic. There, poignant questions, intense thoughts, and murky fears stalked her in isolation as the realities of the war became real to her in a new way.

Would anything of her, that gave her life meaning, be left when this was all over, or were they all merely playing the parts they had been destined to play since before they'd been born?

CHAPTER TWO

PATH OF CHOICES

By the time she finally finished encoding the messages, Norill's entire body ached. The small window and overcast day afforded her precious little light to work with, and both the knowledge of more lost friends and the Nazis unwelcome interest in her weighed heavily on her mind.

She sat back and began to massage the bridge of her nose, temporarily relieving some of the sinus pressure there. Thoughts adrift, her attention was drawn to the window by the sudden sound of raindrops pelting against the glass. She stared absently as the drops alternately stung the glass and traced lazy patterns down the dirty pane.

What if the war had never happened?

Norill calmly breathed and summoned images of the life she would have if the Nazis had never come. Instead of fostering further resentment, the fantasies provided her with a goal —hope. One day the Nazis would be gone, and her dreams would be reality.

They would be, that was, if she lived to see it.

Grimly, she pondered the risk Vinni was asking her to take. Serving as a translator and courier was one thing, but she was not a trained spy. And she was certainly no hero. She was just a common patriot fighting for her country the only way she could during these dark days.

What if she made a mistake?

With resistance cells falling, they could ill-afford her novice efforts endangering another one. The thought of taking on such responsibility weighed heavily on her heart. Still, Vinni must have faith in her abilities or she would never even consider putting them all at such potential peril. Norill absently tapped her pen against the desktop.

Could she actually make a real difference in this horrible war?

Norill's thoughts began to replay flashes of memories involving her friend and mentor. Although they were not family by blood, it felt as if they'd always been a part of each other's lives. Vinni never failed to demonstrate trust in her and Norill had grown and flourished under her love, guidance, and friendship. Her eyes drifted to the grim news contained in the now encoded dispatches she would soon deliver.

Norill sighed. There was but one choice.

Her task completed, and suddenly feeling quite lonely, Norill descended back to the brighter ambiance of the front room and Vinni.

"Finished," Norill announced as she stretched her shoulder muscles to loosen them and consulted a nearby clock. "Oh. I'll be late getting this to the newspaper."

"They'll manage. Haktor was quite upset when he left," Vinni noted as she sipped some tea. "I do worry about him doing something foolish."

"He's too smart for that," Norill said as she straightened her blonde hair into a presentable state. "He's been doing this longer than any of us and survived. He's not about to do something rash now."

"Perhaps," Vinni responded noncommittally but Norill was too distracted to notice.

She turned.

"About earlier …," Norill began but Vinni waved her off.

No apology was necessary between them. Nothing about the current state of the world was easy. They were each doing the best they possibly could. Guided by their fears and their hearts. Norill rested a comforting hand upon the older woman's shoulder.

"Is there anything else you need before I go?"

Vinni pondered the question for a handful of seconds.

"If Gerntz is serious about the lessons, we'd better have more sheet music on hand, particularly German and Austrian composers," she decided. Norill's response would tell her everything she needed to know.

"I'll see what the shop has," Norill assured her before taking her leave.

"Take my umbrella," Vinni bid her student as the young woman departed. "No sense getting all wet."

"Thanks, Vinni. I'll see you tomorrow."

*

The walk down to the bookshop proved rather cumbersome. Norill's heels repeatedly slipped on the wet stones of the street as she attempted to balance the umbrella and the load of precious papers she carried. The struggle grew worse when her right heel unexpectedly lodged itself into a gap between two cobblestones. The unanticipated and abrupt lurch that resulted nearly sent her to the ground.

"Can I help you, Norill?" a familiar voice behind her suddenly asked.

Norill half-turned, not really wanting to acknowledge what she'd have normally taken at face value — a kind offer.

"I think I can manage," she hastily affirmed as she attempted to force the heel free while maintaining her grip on both the umbrella and papers. Norill's efforts proved only marginally successful in the sense that neither she nor her meager but significant belongings fell.

Wordlessly, Sigdis approached, bent down, and pulled upward on Norill's entrapped heel, eventually freeing it.

"Thank you," Norill mechanically said as she hurriedly leaned over to retrieve several papers that had jostled themselves loose from her grasp.

As the women completed picking up the papers, their eyes met for the first time.

Each froze.

They'd grown up on the same street and been friends before the war, quite close in fact during their school years.

Now the unspoken plea in Sigdis's eyes for some kind of connection or understanding frightened Norill. She moved to withdraw; however, her former friend reached out and delicately touched her upper arm.

"I haven't seen you in forever. How have you been?" Sigdis asked, seizing this unforeseen opportunity to talk to her former friend.

"Fine. I'm fine. Thank you for your help," Norill offered a tight smile, fighting the impulse to grab the papers from Sigdis's hand, while shifting away from the woman's light grasp.

The discomfort between them appeared for a heartbeat of seconds on both their faces.

"Your family is well?" Sigdis continued hopefully as they stood, unwilling to allow their interaction to end.

"Yes, yes, we're all quite well," Norill assured her, knowing she was going nowhere until she could regain all her now dampened papers.

Even though they appeared to be nothing more than sheet music, the fact that Sigdis held the encoded communiqués caused Norill's pulse to involuntarily quicken. This young woman's choices, and those of her family, sickened Norill. Ever since the invasion, they had publicly supported both the Nazi occupiers and the policies of the Norwegian puppet government under Quisling.

They'd welcomed Nazis into their tavern and hotel, where Sigdis had worked since she was a teenager. Undoubtedly, that's where she'd become involved with the Nazi officer to whom she was now openly his mistress.

In Norill's eyes, Sigdis and her family represented the worst of the occupation. They were collaborators and traitors: feared, loathed, and mistrusted. They'd reputedly even provided the Nazis with the names of several Jewish community members who had not been seen in some time.

These choices afforded Sigdis and her family all types of special freedoms and resources denied to most Norwegian citizens under the Nazi occupation. It also, for the time being, protected them from direct reprisals.

But outside the Nazi sphere of influence, they were pariahs, fallen people, who most community members viewed as beyond redemption. To have been seen even talking to Sigdis like this was sure to elicit Norill censure from the community.

"Still taking lessons with Vinni?" Sigdis pressed as she glanced down at the papers in her hand.

"Yes."

Norill felt breathless and Sigdis perceived her own efforts were getting her nowhere. She relented.

"Okay. Well, it was good seeing you again," Sigdis smiled bravely as she held out Norill's papers.

As she reached for them Norill was caught off guard by Sigdis suddenly pulling her very close.

"I never had a choice," her fallen friend painfully declared as she leaned in and hugged Norill, who stood stock still.

Sigdis pulled back, gazed apologetically one last time upon Norill before backing away and disappearing up a side street.

*

Dazed by her encounter, Norill numbly wandered down the remainder of the hill. Talking to Sigdis had left her shaken. She was a vivid reminder of what fate might await Norill if she did as Vinni advised and allowed the Nazi to pursue her.

Her thoughts drifted to childhood. To playing hide-and-seek with Sigdis and the other kids at school. Smiling. Laughing. Reveling in the innocent thrill of the game. Friends.

But that was a long time ago. Her musings broadened to

the faces of others who'd played those games. How many would she never see again because of this war? Because of people like Sigdis and her new … friends. The game they all now played was one she must win.

Norill quickened her pace.

Within minutes she reached the main town square near the harbor. An assortment of shops, cafes, and restaurants framed a green space that was dotted with sparse trees, a few benches, and that stretched down to the water of the fjord. The streets were a mix of those walking, on bikes, and an assortment of vehicles; including, unfortunately, many used by Nazi troops and officers.

Norill could feel unseen eyes scrutinizing her. She shivered involuntarily as she made a final turn before stepping into the Ericksons' bookshop.

Fighting the urge to lock the door to keep the world out of her quiet place of employment, she instead deposited Vinni's borrowed umbrella behind the cash register desk and took an instant to smooth her skirt. Momentarily refreshed, she gathered up her papers and headed down one of the aisles and toward the back of the store.

The quiet was shattered almost immediately.

"I didn't think you were ever going to get here," Tekla fussed, as she got down from a step stool.

Norill smiled.

Tekla was close to forty, but her diminutive size and youthful features often made her seem much younger. She also tended to talk rapidly and even before the war was a bit of a nervous wreck.

Her next flurry of words illustrated this perfectly.

"Mr. Erickson kept asking me if you were coming in today and I kept telling him I didn't know and he kept asking so I'm glad you're here, so he'll stop asking," Tekla quickly explained as she adjusted her glasses. "Oh my, I hadn't even noticed it was raining again. So much rain this year. Much more rain than we normally get, but you know I've always liked the rain. It's not so bad once you get used to it. Good for the growing season too."

Tekla paused only long enough to draw in a deep breath before continuing.

"Now you need to finish re-shelving the back part of the fiction section. I think I left off in the M's. Mr. Erickson said the cookbooks can wait … and hey, where are you going?"

"The water closet. I'll be right back," Norill promised as she strategically extricated herself.

As much as she liked Tekla, the resistance dispatches could not wait. As Vinni often reminded her, "Lives are lost to time."

The bookshop was partially housed in what had once been someone's home. Actually, the ramshackle structure was a combination of what had once been several individual buildings. To that end, an old laundry chute still existed in the back hallway near the restroom.

As she approached, Norill extracted a blend of pages with braille notation and sheet music from her stacks of paper and dropped them into the chute. Relieved to have made her delivery, she exhaled a sigh before removing herself from her coat and did her best to set about her regular duties at the bookshop.

**

"Just a minute," the voice on the other side of the door announced in response to Norill's repeated knock.

"Did you save me some lunch this time?" Norill asked unfazed.

There was only the briefest of pauses.

"All these years and you still expect me to make you

lunch?" her brother joked as he opened the door. "And on such a nice day."

Norill hugged her older brother. As usual he offered a friendly but detached embrace back.

"Happy birthday, Rejor! I suppose since it's your birthday, I'll let you off the hook and buy you lunch," she offered.

"What about dinner?" he countered. "Kador just called and wants me to meet him and the others along the waterfront for some games and a drink."

"Oh, I see. Too good for lunch with your little sister. All right, dinner it is but I'm giving you your gift now."

"It never seems to do me any good when I argue with you. Come in," Rejor invited as he backed away from the door. "That sun sure feels nice. Those rainy days last week got old."

"Are you playing cards again with the guys?" Norill asked as she entered, and he closed the door behind her. She hoped the inquiry sounded casual, but she was well aware of the financial and social problems her brother's gambling habit had produced over the years.

"Probably but I think they resent playing with my deck. Bet they think I'm cheating. Must be why they keep trying to get me to play bocce. Sometimes I think games are the only thing that make life worth anything. We shall have to play a game one-day, dear sister. Say, you're in a good mood," her brother noted. "Did your Nazi admirer fail to show up again?"

"Second Tuesday in a row," she gushed. "Hopefully, they shipped him off somewhere else," Norill added as she set her bag on the nearby table.

Rejor nodded.

"God willing, he'll never show up. And you haven't seen him in public lately either, not at any of the checkpoints around town, just gone?"

Norill shook her head.

"It appears so," she could hear the relief in her own voice.

Haktor had made some preliminary arrangements for her to leave and visit fake relatives if needed, but Gerntz's repeated absences were making such considerations less likely. The situation had also enabled her to have a few private conversations with Haktor about how she might go about gaining his trust and eventually any useful information if the Nazi did come. Norill was still dubious such efforts would yield positive outcomes but at least she felt a bit more prepared.

"Fate is smiling upon you, sister," Rejor grinned. "Father's always said you're destined to be fortunate."

Although he tried to mask it, Norill could detect the hint of bitterness that accompanied these words. Her brother's demons were always lurking just beneath the surface. Maybe, one day, he would open up to her more about them. Rejor could be a hard person to love but she did love him. She hesitated before making the offer.

"If you ever want to talk about Lisbeth …"

Rejor's countenance grew darker at the mention of his wife's name. He offered only a curt nod of refusal, forcing Norill to refocus.

She returned to the present.

"From the latest Allied messages, I translated, it sounds like they are moving again in Northern Africa."

"I'll look forward to reading more tomorrow when I go back to the newspaper." Rejor replied. "Except for making my delivery they gave me today off."

"You deserve it," Norill rubbed his arm in support. He didn't normally like being touched by surprise, but he often allowed her to do so without reproach. She was family he trusted.

They paused a moment.

"Speaking of reading, I was having some problems with

one of your braille codes the other day," he stated but made no attempt to sit down, clearly wanting to keep their visit brief.

"Sorry, I had to prepare more sheet music for Vinni, and I was in a hurry to leave in case that Nazi showed up for his lessons," Norill admitted.

Better for Vinni to try and get a read on him before Norill attempted any subterfuge. In his own fisherman's parlance, Haktor had basically given the same advice. Let Vinni do the real fishing and keep Norill dangling as bait on the hook to keep the Nazi coming back.

If he ever even showed up again.

"This guy's sure got you spooked. I taught you better than that when it comes to your resistance work. I figured those messages out, but you can't get sloppy. Lives could be lost if we aren't careful. Besides, I don't want to ever risk having you come to the newspaper or to bring any materials here for clarification," Rejor told her.

It was Rejor who'd taught her both braille and the coding system they used. His "newspaper" was, in fact, an illegal publication, produced and printed in secret, which kept the public informed about what was really happening in the war much to the consternation of the Nazi propaganda machine and Quisling's manipulations of the public.

The paper also filtered and shared communications from listening outposts like the cell Norill was involved in. It was so invaluable that even Norill wasn't sure where exactly or how broad Rejor's operation was, only that she was to use the chute in the bookshop to deliver materials to him.

"I know. I know. I'll pay more attention," she promised.

"You mentioned a present?" he finally reminded her after an awkward silence.

Norill retrieved a fair-sized tin from her bag.

"Smell," she directed, removing the lid.

He smiled.

"How did you manage to get this much sugar?" Rejor wondered aloud as he clasped the tin.

"You have your secrets and I have mine. War rationing be damned. Happy birthday," she said again, taking her brother's free hand and squeezing it.

Rejor had grown more distant since the outbreak of the war and Norill worried that the stress of running the paper was making him harsher. Well, that and the unresolved fate of Lisbeth.

"Thank you."

"I'll let you get on with your day then. Dinner tonight?"

"I'll meet you at the café by your bookshop around six," he agreed.

"Can I tell Mother to meet us?"

Rejor hesitated as he opened the door.

"If you like," he conceded, as one of his fingers tapped abrasively against the sugar tin.

**

Although she heard the front doorbell jingle, Norill did not stir, engrossed completely in a book she had stumbled upon. She loved to read, to learn. Both the war and her finances had closed a path to higher learning to her. But here she was free of those constraints. It was part of the appeal to this job.

She knew Mr. Erickson would disapprove of her attitude toward whomever had just arrived in the store, but he'd left early, and Tekla was too absorbed with sorting the stockroom to notice her minor indiscretion. She rarely felt this relaxed, and oftentimes customers wandered off into the far corners of the store in search of whatever literary prize they sought without ever acknowledging a greeting from whoever was behind the sales counter.

"*Guten tag*. Norill, yes?"

The fingers that had been absentmindedly twisting a strand of her hair froze mid-motion, and her heart quickened as Norill's eyes rose from the book and gazed into those of the Nazi soldier, Gerntz. The voiceless exchange felt endless as her emotions and thoughts surged in several directions at once.

"What are you reading?" he finally asked, breaking the stalemate.

Norill straightened herself defensively on her stool behind the counter, closed the book, and set it aside facedown.

"May I help you?" she coolly inquired.

"You may," Gerntz replied, undeterred. "I should like to find more sheet music for my next lesson tomorrow."

A host of questions flooded Norill's mind, but she kept them to herself. To ask would only invite further conversation with this man and that was to be avoided at all costs. She pointed in the direction of the sheet music.

"Could you please show me?" the Nazi inclined his head toward her.

Almost as if she was dreaming, Norill slowly stood, self-consciously smoothed the front of her skirt, and walked him toward the back of the shop to the music. Every nerve in her body seemed to vibrate. And with each step further away from the front windows her fears grew more pronounced. She half expected his friends to appear any moment and corner her.

"Here," she softly announced when they at last reached the shelved pile of sheet music.

She brushed past him, intent on escaping to the front of the bookstore, but suddenly found herself restrained. The presence of his hand on her wrist was fleeting and far from harsh, but she drew her arm back toward her body as if she had been delivered a strong electric shock.

They were so close she couldn't help but inhale the scent of his aftershave.

"I would appreciate you selecting some moderate level material for me," he politely requested.

His blue eyes afforded her no refuge. Norill turned from them and attempted to concentrate on locating music.

She could sense his gaze upon her as he studied her form and every motion she made. A part of her wanted to flee but she dare not try. Instead, Norill retreated inward, filling her head with music as she worked. If she didn't, his closeness, the burning awareness of her isolation, and the knowledge that had passed between their eyes would overwhelm her.

"Your friend thinks very highly of you," Gerntz remarked as she pulled several sheets from the stack.

"Mrs. Naess is a generous woman," Norill at last responded, managing to keep her voice from quaking. "Eight selections should be more than adequate."

She offered him the papers.

"Undoubtedly, but I speak of Fräulein Sigdis Karlsen," he clarified.

Norill lost her purchase on the sheet music she'd pulled as a door near them suddenly opened.

"Oh dear, sorry, Norill. I should have called out first. This always seems to happen, it's like we have our own traditions in this shop. My, I could have spent another six hours working in that stockroom and it would still be a disaster. Here, I'll get those; it's the least I can do," Tekla declared as she snatched up the scattered sheet music from the floor.

"Finish up for me," Norill bid as she retreated further back into the shop without looking back to see Tekla's reaction when she turned around and discovered Gerntz, whom she had yet to notice standing behind her.

*

Norill was angry as she turned the lock on the door to the water closet. She hated the Nazis. She hated all collaborators and Sigdis for talking about her. And she especially hated Gerntz.

She glared at her reflection. Fleeing here made Norill feel weak, and more than anything, she hated that he'd made her feel controlled and weak.

Gerntz's lack of attendance to his first two lessons provided Vinni the perfect excuse to refuse to teach him. Yet, apparently, she hadn't.

Could she have sent him here deliberately to look for sheet music, fostering Gerntz's interest in her? Was this a test?

The eyes of the reflection lost some of their fire. They changed again as a new, unpleasant thought entered her consciousness.

How did Gerntz know about her connection to Sigdis?

Aside from their spontaneous encounter a few weeks previous, Norill hadn't had any interactions with the other woman in quite some time. Could Sigdis have been following her? Worse still, had Gerntz been following her that day, witnessed their meeting, and investigated her relationship with Norill's former friend further?

Norill's blood was now ice.

Why did Gerntz pursue her?

He wanted something from her very badly. The image of his intense blue eyes hung before her. Did he intend to violate her? Force her into a relationship with him? Arrest and torture her and the other members of the resistance cell?

Her mind recoiled at the horrible images set loose upon her frantic mind.

Reason fought back against these questions and phantoms. First thing in the morning, she would insist that Haktor use his contacts to get her safely out of town, without raising suspicions. Leaving would protect her and the resistance.

Unconsciously, the reflection nodded back to her and Norill took a deep breath. She could hear the church bells outside calling the bottom of the hour. The sound recalled her thoughts to the present.

Soon it would be time to meet Rejor for dinner. Wait. She'd completely forgotten about telling their mother. The safest course was to go home. But then again, she could not abandon Rejor on his birthday, and there was no guarantee she would be able to reach him by phone. She'd have to wait for him at the café.

"Everything all right?" Tekla asked when Norill at last re-emerged from the back.

"I think it was something from lunch," Norill lied. "Thank you for dealing with that ..."

"Jack-booted moron is what he is. Man doesn't know his Beethoven from his Mozart. Piano lessons, cultural experts, huh. And these Nazis want to conquer the world? Well, what can you expect from a witless goon anyway?" Tekla ranted. "I tell you Mrs. Naess is going to have her hands full."

Norill couldn't help but laugh at Tekla's tirade and soon they were both laughing uproariously.

"Did he say anything else?" Norill asked, hoping for another diatribe by Tekla.

The shorter woman collected herself before answering.

"Only that he liked the shop and would be back," Tekla rolled her eyes.

Suddenly Norill felt much more sober.

"Bad enough they're out there. Let's just hope we don't have this place crawling with Nazis next," Tekla shook her head as she turned the door sign to close the shop for the day, missing her co-worker's troubled expression.

*

The spoon pinged against the ceramic cup as Norill rescued the saturated tea bag from the steaming contents it had created. Church bells chimed again.

Where was Rejor?

Even though it was a pleasant evening, there seemed to be few people out. If he didn't arrive soon, they'd have to worry about curfew.

Norill drew her jacket closer and carefully raised the cup full of hot tea to her lips. As she did so her eyes scanned the square, fearful any moment Gerntz would reappear. Norill had strategically set herself at the outdoor table she considered least visible to most of the square. If only Tekla had been able to stay, at least she wouldn't be waiting here alone.

It happened so abruptly that for an instant all she did was blink. Without warning a man, whom she'd never set eyes on before, was suddenly seated across from her.

For a moment, they simply stared at each other.

"You work in the bookshop?" he asked with only a slight accent.

Norill mechanically nodded.

"My wife loves Ibsen," he hastily declared.

"'*The strongest man in the world is he who stands most alone,*'" Norill responded after looking to verify that no one was close by.

"I love Shakespeare," she added.

"'*So wise so young, they say, do never live long.*'" The man's thick beard hid most of his face, but his sharp eyes relaxed for just an instant.

"I'm sure the shop can help you at eight tomorrow morning," Norill nervously took a sip of tea as the man vanished from her sight.

To the casual observer, she presented the demeanor of a woman happy for the simple pleasure of quietly finishing a cup of tea after a long day's work. But Norill fought to keep the cup in her hand from shaking as her pulse raced.

Somewhere out there a group of British commandos needed her help. They needed her aid so desperately they'd risked sending someone to speak to her in public. Norill dropped money on the table and started her journey home, uncertain if she was truly capable of saving anyone—including herself.

CHAPTER THREE

AGENTS OF THE FIFTH COLUMN

Norill jumped down and gasped for air as she and Tekla were overcome by a haze of dust that wafted down upon them from the top of the shelf.

"I've got to get some water," Tekla managed as she lurched away from Norill who was still coughing. Norill wiped her tearing eyes with her sleeve and wordlessly accepted the second glass of water Tekla returned with a few minutes later.

"That was a bad one," the short woman noted as she fully regained her breath.

"I hate when he makes us clean these stacks back here," Norill said as Tekla nodded in concurrence.

"He's the tall one, shouldn't he be back here doing this?"

Tekla had barely finished uttering her complaint when the shop's owner, Mr. Erickson, suddenly rounded the corner. Mere seconds after his abrupt appearance, he began to sneeze uncontrollably until he retrieved a handkerchief to cover his mouth and nose.

"Good Lord! Look at this. It'll take until doomsday to clear all this dust out of here," he bluntly asserted as his sharp eyes fixed on the mass of dust roiling through a nearby spot of light. "Get some of these windows opened."

"They're painted shut," Tekla reminded him before withering under Mr. Erickson's annoyed gaze and returned to her dusting.

"You have a phone call," the shop owner informed Norill.

"Do you know who it is?" she asked, wondering if the British commando from the café last night could be foolish or desperate enough to call her. He still had not shown up this morning.

"Your mother," Mr. Erickson told her as he lowered the obscuring piece of cloth from his face. "She's quite upset. Use the phone up front."

Norill hastened to the shop's checkout counter, darted behind it, and grabbed the phone's receiver.

"Mother, are you there? What's wrong?"

At first all she heard was the sound of heavy breathing and muffled voices shouting in the background. Then a series of loud bangs erupted through the speaker.

"Norill, they're taking it. They're taking it all," her mother's trembling voice asserted before the line went dead.

"Hello? Mother? Mother?!" Norill's heart was thundering in her ears so loudly she never heard her coworker's approach.

"What is it? What's going on?" Tekla asked, startling Norill. "Do you need help?"

"I need your bike," Norill stammered as her mind and fears drove in a host of conflicting directions.

"It's parked out front," Tekla declared, nervously wringing her hands, anxious to gain some insight into her friend's plight.

She would gain none as Norill stiffened upon noticing Mr. Erickson making his way back toward them. She could not afford to be detained. Her tension eased momentarily as he was forced to pause, stopped by a customer with an interest in obtaining rare books about Norse mythology.

Norill pivoted her attention back to Tekla and spoke rapidly.

"A man reserved a copy of *Enemy of the People* last night. I've set it aside for him behind the front counter. It has a blue bookmark sticking out from the top. If he comes for it, tell him I'll be back."

Without uttering another word, Norill grabbed her handbag, left the shop, retrieved Tekla's bicycle, and began to furiously pedal. Her family's farm was several kilometers outside of town. Aside from the Nazi checkpoints, she only paused once before leaving town, witnessing a sight that temporarily brought both her mind and motions to an abrupt halt.

There in the street stood Haktor openly talking with Sigdis as Nazi soldiers lingered nearby. Realizing the folly of such an astonished reaction in public, she suppressed the discord within and resumed her rhythmic motions.

*

Unwilling to allow any manifestation of weakness, Norill fought to suppress the urge to massage the muscles in her arms that had been strained by the soldiers' harsh grip. Instead, she tacitly crossed her arms. She'd been seized by the Germans immediately upon her arrival and now languished pensively along the side of the road as the guards radioed their superiors regarding her presence.

Her family's farm was at once neither near nor far from town. This was a land blessed with a richness of herbs and wildflowers during warmer months, a rolling blend of both grassland and mighty stands of timber, a place where the sunlight held memories of searching for wild berries and the sound of murmuring streams. But the incongruous nature of the scene before her drove home harsh realities.

The normally tranquil environment of her childhood home was abuzz with all manner of mechanized monsters and uniformed men who projected wariness, menace, and a coldness this place never knew even in the cruelest of winters. And this was a sight now playing out daily across her occupied homeland in any number of places: in homes, farms, and villages just like hers.

"Come," one of her guards directly bid as he replaced the radio receiver on its cradle.

Norill hesitated only long enough to retrieve Tekla's bike then slowly walked the remainder of her journey flanked closely by two uniformed intruders she would gladly see destroyed.

Each progressive step she took revealed new, unwelcome truths.

Numerous eyes along the road and lengthy driveway tracked her every motion as her measured pace brought her ever closer to home. A nest of vipers would have been less unnerving. All was noise and motion as motor engines roared, orders were shouted, and gun wielding soldiers moved hurriedly to follow them.

As they rounded the final curve and rose beyond the obscuring trees, Norill's destination finally lay before her.

Both the modest home, barn, and supply buildings were being turned inside out. Nazi vehicles now brimmed with familiar items from the house, crops, supplies, even animals stolen from the farm. In fact, items were still being tossed out of the open windows of the structures.

Norill's agitation rose. Right now, none of this mattered, only determining her mother's fate.

"Halt," a crisp, authoritarian voice behind them crisply commanded, bringing Norill and her armed companions to an abrupt cessation.

"*Spricht sie Deutsch*?" the officer asked the guards as he approached, scrutinizing Norill for any shred of information he could gather from her appearance.

"*Sie hat keener gesprochen,*" one of the men reported.

The officer nodded, switching effortlessly to Norwegian.

"I understand you live here, Miss?"

"Haugen. And my mother lives here. I have rooms in town. What brings you to our farm?" Norill inquired, matching his tone.

"Why the war, naturally."

His amused smile only added to his insulting tone as he needlessly pulled at the cuffs of his gloves before proceeding. "I believe this document should clarify our purpose."

The narrow-faced man withdrew an envelope from his

jacket, which he then offered to the helpless woman for inspection. Both Norill's breathing and her heart grew heavier as she read, but there was no mistaking her father's signature on the paper. Challenging its validity with the officer before her was pointless, especially as it was plain how much he was relishing her shock.

She would not give him the satisfaction of protesting.

"Where is my mother?" Norill asked quietly as she returned the document to the smug man.

"You may come back this afternoon for her," the officer declared dismissively as he clicked his heels and politely inclined his head in mock respect.

Norill's eyes wavered across the front of the house, seeking any sign of her mother's presence, but, for some reason, they fixed on her parents' open bedroom window where the curtains blew outward, carried by the winds. Rough hands were again clasping her, directing her motions in the opposite direction from her mind's will.

She stiffened, attempting to stay in place.

"Conduct Miss Haugen back to town. Send an escort this afternoon when we're ready," the unsympathetic officer ordered his guards before directing his parting affront to Norill. "Your family's sacrifice to the Reich's war effort is greatly appreciated. Good day."

*

Another metallic ping sounded off behind Norill as her bicycle's tire rim again encountered the car's trunk. This time the clash of metal beckoned Norill from her anguished reverie. They were over halfway back to town and she could not afford to be seen arriving in a Nazi staff car, much less return to the bookstore and risk leading the Germans directly to the commandos.

“I’m going to be sick. Stop the car. Stop the car!” she insisted as a familiar sight loomed into view as they rounded a bend in the road.

Apparently, her remaining guard was unwilling to test her claim while they were in the car and ordered the driver to pull over. Norill struggled past the guard and within seconds of exiting the vehicle wretched on the nearby churchyard fence and her clothing. She ignored the men’s derisive laughter at her temporary incapacity. It was better that they believe her to be feeble.

They lit cigarettes but made no move to offer any assistance as they idly began to talk amongst themselves.

“I should like to remain at the church,” Norill finally requested.

The guard’s quick eyes surveyed both her and the modest but unique stave style church[3], which was surrounded inside the fence by clusters of steepled grave markers. The multiple gabled, wooden roofs of the church rose artistically upward and were adorned with decorative embellishments and assorted carvings.

The man’s cool gaze returned to hers as he motioned for her to return to the staff car. He had orders to return her to town, and this place was only halfway to his objective. Norill shook her head in mute protest. He took an aggressive step toward her.

“May I be of assistance?” a voice unexpectedly invited from the other side of the fence.

The middle-aged clergyman lowered his gloved hands as the Nazi guard relaxed the posture of the gun he’d reflectively retrieved. The two men conversed out of earshot for several minutes before the guard grabbed Tekla’s bicycle from the car’s trunk and tossed it to the ground as the clergyman

---

3 Stave churches were wooden structures built during the Middle Ages in the Scandinavian regions and Northern Europe

offered the Nazi a proper salute. The car's tires shrouded Norill in a cloud of dust before departing.

"You're fortunate I was out gardening. I volunteered to be your temporary guardian. Convinced them it would be less hassle than driving you to and from town all day. They insist you remain here until they return for you. I hope that's agreeable," the clergyman explained as he stooped to help Norill to her feet.

She politely nodded but refused to meet the man's eye. Grateful as she was, she needed to think, not endure his curiosity.

Norill drew Tekla's abused bicycle inside the fence, and then followed her benefactor into the back of the church where she accepted the glass of water he offered her. She took a brief pause to refresh herself in the modest water closet before joining the clergyman in the main church.

"May comforting thoughts find you here," the man wished before retreating back outside to continue his work.

It was quiet here. Peaceful.

Norill's body settled heavily onto one of the pews. The events of the past hour assaulting her emotions with unimaginable fears and harsh realities.

How much more would they take from her?

Why did that letter exist? Her father would never have willingly signed over their farm. Was he now dead? She hadn't seen him since the morning of the second day of the Nazi invasion over two years ago. His face a delicate echo in her memory. How would she tell her mother? Would she see her again?

Her mind should have been focused on finding answers.

What should she do?

She must do something.

But instead, her thoughts were filled by the silence of the ancient wooden structure, becoming one with it as the shadows slowly changed position in accordance with the sunlight flowing through both the stained-glass windows and open entryway.

A fleeting remembrance of attending services here as a child graced her thoughts. She'd been happier then. At least, until the untimely passing of her young sister.

A pang of guilt overcame her. She should have visited her grave in the churchyard more often. Could she even still find the marker?

Norill's connection to church had always been tenuous. She possessed a dim memory of this being different prior to Rejor's blindness in childhood but that was a lifetime ago. Now even Norway's Church could offer little in the way of solace as Quisling and his Nazi masters claimed it for their own nefarious purposes. Another piece of Norway captured, co-opted, beset by willing agents of the fifth column[4]. The longer the occupation continued the more numerous the ranks of the corrupted grew.

Trust was becoming a deadly commodity.

The image of Haktor and Sigdis speaking burned in her mind. To the best of her knowledge, they had no reason to interact and Haktor was the last person who would want to be seen with a known Nazi collaborator. But an unnerving pattern of Sigdis suddenly speaking to those close to Norill was beginning to form. First Gerntz and now him.

Had Haktor been compromised?

With the suppression of Norwegian culture, secretive nature of the resistance, and hidden nature of collaborators one never knew now who sided with whom. If the war didn't tear them all apart, all the secrets and lies would.

What kind of a future could she ever hope to build in such a reality?

---

4 Employing agents to subvert a nation's unity from within by misinformation, espionage, and other subterfuge.

Norill quietly studied her hands.

Would she ever know love before she died?

A helmeted shadow suddenly hovered before her, backlit in the church's entryway.

"Come," the familiar, unwelcome voice of her guard starkly ordered.

Norill lingered for several heartbeats under the oppressive presence of the guard's shadow. Inwardly, she feared the next minutes to come as the doubts and fears of her imagination attempted to anticipate the unknown reality that waited. Her eyes were drawn to the stains of sickness left on her dress.

Maybe she was weak.

She stirred as the impatient shadow did and together, they exited the church.

There was no trace of the gardening clergyman other than several freshly planted beds of flowers that now graced the fence line. Tekla's bicycle had apparently already been loaded into one of the two Nazi staff cars that idled along the side of the road. She was conducted to the first car but to Norill's surprise when the door opened, it was the sight of the Nazi officer from the farm who greeted her.

"Miss Haugen. Here to bare your soul, perhaps?"

Norill could not suppress her emotions in time as he rose to tower over her.

"Where is my mother?" she desperately demanded.

"In the rear car," the officer absently gestured. "Tell me, what do you know of the downed Allied glider we located on her property?"

The man's eyes bore deeply into Norill as the question hung between them.

Her gaze was drawn to the death's head emblem on the front of his cap. She could sense the closeness of the guard behind her. Norill's mouth felt dry as she truthfully responded.

"Nothing."

The officer made no move to break his intense visual interrogation.

"Interesting. Your mother claims the same excuse. I wonder how it is that such a glaring oversight is possible, especially as there is suggestive evidence that Allied soldiers sheltered in the barn."

"Where did it crash? When? How far from the house?" Norill challenged in rapid succession.

A disquieting smile spread across the officer's face.

"I'm releasing your mother into your custody, Miss Haugen. For how long is entirely up to you for I will have the truth. Obtain it for me soon or rest assured I will and somehow I doubt you'll approve of my methods when I do."

The earnestness in his voice was chilling.

"How can I clear her name if you're already convinced she's guilty?" Norill protested as the officer sat back down in the car.

"Your driver has instructions to return you to town. When you have something, tell him and he will contact me."

The guard pulled Norill back from the car, which pulled away seconds later. She wordlessly followed the man to the second car and offered no resistance as he opened the door.

As promised, her mother was there.

The older woman made no effort to look at her daughter as she sat down. A lone suitcase sat between them. The car sank a little lower as the guard assumed the seat next to the driver and forcibly shut the door. The only sound that filled the void was that of the idling engine.

"Where am I to drive you, Norill?"

Her heart sank lower. Of course, he was here. She closed her eyes and clenched her jaw as she bitterly answered.

"Take us to Mrs. Naess please, Gerntz."

*

The return journey was interminable.

Norill longed to break her shared silence with her mother but she dared not as the Nazi staff car slowly wove through town in pursuit of its ultimate destination. Had Gerntz been instructed to parade them past as many judgmental eyes as possible or was this his own twisted torment?

They seemed to visit every single checkpoint.

There'd been no need to drive into the very heart of town but here they were for all to see. Still, she barely allowed herself to take notice of the stares and condescending looks of those they drove slowly past. She didn't even respond to Gerntz's stolen glances at her as he talked to the guard or adjusted the rearview mirror.

What would her mother tell her about the Allied glider and its crew?

Norill became lost to memory. In it, she was drowning, just as she emotionally was now. The ice had broken that day and had her father not reacted quickly she'd have slid beneath the frozen mass forever. The haunting image of the impenetrable, watery infinity consumed her, as it had since that day. A living death. Her breath grew short.

The water was something to fear.

So transfixed had she become by the black leather of the seat in front of her that she failed at first to notice their arrival at Vinni's house.

Coming here was a risk, but less it seemed than having Gerntz take Norill to the rooms she rented in town or to the bookshop. Her mind raced as she calculated the dangers of bringing her mother here.

Vinni she could trust. By now she was as much a mother to Norill as the woman who sat beside her in this wretched Nazi staff car. But what of Haktor?

The disturbing image of Haktor speaking with Sigdis suddenly returned as the door next to her mother was opened by Gerntz. The Nazi soldier courteously helped the older woman out of the car before leaning in to retrieve her suitcase.

Norill met his eye.

"If either of you attempt to leave town you will be shot," he plainly stated.

Norill solemnly nodded once before looking away. The deadly intensity of his tone afforded her no illusions regarding his warning.

As he withdrew, the guard opened Norill's door and motioned her out. Tekla's bicycle was propped near the steps to Vinni's front door and beside it, her mother, flanked by Gerntz, who carried her suitcase, waited for her.

Norill took a moment to regard the uniformed man.

Who had he been before the war?

The thought flashed through Norill's mind quickly but nonetheless caught her off guard. She buried it as she knocked and awaited Vinni.

"Who is it?"

"Hello, Vinni, may Mother and I come in for a short time?" Norill calmly asked when the blind musician answered her summons.

Vinni hesitated, clearly distracted as she perceived the presence of others beyond those Norill had mentioned waiting outside.

"I … didn't forget an appointment did I, Norill?" she softly asked.

"No, Vinni," Norill struggled to keep her voice from trembling. "Gerntz is here to drop off Mother's bag and then he'll be leaving."

"I see. Give me a moment, won't you," said Vinni as she closed the door.

"Do you wish me to drive you to the bookshop later?"

Gerntz asked.

"No," she managed without turning to face him but inclined her head wordlessly toward Tekla's bicycle just as the door swung open.

Norill's heart sank.

"Hello Norill, Mrs. Haugen," Sigdis cordially greeted them as she finished putting on her gloves. "Nice that it isn't raining today, yes? Excuse me."

"Indeed," Norill breathed in disbelief as she stepped aside to allow Sigdis to pass, who nodded politely to Gerntz.

"Thank you again for the tea, Mrs. Naess," Sigdis called as she waved farewell to Vinni who'd reappeared in the doorway.

Vinni offered a short wave in response.

"Always nice when former students visit," she commented as she moved to allow the others inside. "I'll get you both some tea as well."

Gerntz placed the suitcase just inside the door before closing it behind the women.

Mother and daughter sat together. The only sounds in the room were the ticking of a clock and that of water being drawn in the kitchen.

Without a word, Norill wrapped her arms around her mother. Their embrace was comforting, reassuring.

"Are you all right?" Norill finally asked as she released the older woman from her grasp.

"Why do you know that Nazi?" her mother responded, her tone rife with suspicion.

"He comes here for lessons from Vinni," Norill incredulously countered, folding her arms. "Nothing more."

Unconvinced, Norill's mother sat down and retrieved her cigarettes and matches. The tea kettle began whistling as she exhaled a measure of smoke from her first cigarette in hours.

"And will you turn me back over to your friend?" her

mother demanded as she flung a spent match into the ashtray on the coffee table. "That SS officer who stole my farm would certainly be impressed."

Why was her mother picking this fight?

"If you have so little faith in me why did you call?" Norill retorted.

"As if Rejor would have come," her mother harshly noted.

"I don't know which of you is worse about that. You know he would have come," Norill affirmed as she rose, checked outside the window, then settled in a chair across from her mother.

The older woman looked away from her daughter.

Despite her anger, Norill could recognize the vulnerability and fear etched on her mother's features. The image of the Nazi document bearing her father's signature flashed through her mind. But the telling marks of stress on her mother's face made it clear that now was not the time to mention it. Afterall, waiting to tell her would do nothing to alter the fact that her father was either dead or that they were helpless to aid him. For now, she alone must carry the burden of this knowledge.

"Sigdis' presence here does not inspire confidence," the woman admitted to her child.

"No … it doesn't," Norill agreed in agitation as she rose to join Vinni in the kitchen.

"Do you need a hand?" Norill asked Vinni as she opened the kitchen door.

The question caused the other woman to lose her purchase on the cup in her hand, which shattered upon the floor.

"Don't move," Norill ordered as she surveyed where the jagged fragments had landed.

"Dammit. So clumsy. Was that the blue one?" Vinni inquired as she nervously wrung her hands together.

"I'm afraid so," Norill observed as she stooped and began to pick up the shards. "Sorry that I startled you."

"Yes," Vinni absently remarked. "Tell me, is there much to clean up?"

"It'll only take a minute," her younger friend assured her. "Mother's farm has been taken by the Nazis for the greater glory of the Third Reich. I need to talk to Rejor. Would you mind if she stays here a few hours while I make arrangements?"

"Dear. No, no of course not," Vinni replied. "Poor woman."

"Is Haktor here?" Norill casually probed.

"What? No. I mean, I've not seen him since this morning. He wasn't here long," Vinni added.

"Hhhmm. Well, I think I've got the last of it," Norill declared as she regained her feet. "It's safe for you to move now. Did he mention any communiqués needing translated?"

Vinni crossed the room to retrieve the tea tray she'd been assembling.

"I think we're one cup short. And we'll need the sugar cubes," she decided.

Norill moved to gather the final items and placed them on the tray.

"Vinni. Did Haktor mention translations?" Norill repeated.

The old music teacher paused in reflection.

"No, not that I recall, but you can go and check if he left anything," she suggested as she prepared to pick up the tea tray.

"Are you all right, Vinni?" Norill queried as she pondered her obviously troubled mentor.

Her friend lingered and lowered her head an instant before raising it and stating, "Don't ask me about Sigdis. It's my business."

"Are we compromised?"

Vinni turned her blank eyes to Norill, but the harsh expression she wore rebuffed her protégé. She raised the tray and vacated the kitchen.

*

It took Norill an extra twenty minutes to make her way back to the bookshop. Surely, she must be under Nazi surveillance of some type. But her meager efforts of pausing and doubling back to expose her watchers proved fruitless.

Her stomach rumbled with hunger, suddenly keenly aware of the paltry amount of food she'd eaten today. Her mind fixated briefly on how wonderful eating some *laks* and *geitost*[5] sounded right now.

Norill's thoughts returned to the tense hour she'd spent with her mother and Vinni. They'd shared little conversation, each lost in their own problems.

Still, Norill hated to leave.

If possible, she'd gladly forgo this trip, but she needed to return Tekla's bicycle and ascertain if the commandos had attempted to contact her. For reasons she couldn't really explain to herself, she's neglected to inform Vinni of the Allied solder's mysterious contact. Undoubtedly, her growing sense of unease regarding Sigdis and the inner turmoil regarding the situation with her mother each played a role. Perhaps it was best to wait and see what developed first.

As she traveled, Norill could not help but feel as if every soul she passed viewed her with suspicion. Halfway to her destination, it began to mist, and she took the opportunity to don a concealing scarf. The hunger pangs worsened as she pedaled, and the stone surfaces grew slick, slowing her further. When at last she drew near her goal, Norill decided to walk the remaining paces.

5 Salmon and sweet semi-hard cheese

Unwilling to endure additional scrutiny in the town square, she opted to approach the bookshop from the rear. Built into a hillside, the exposed basement always made the shop look much larger than it actually was from this perspective. Leaving the bicycle down here and making her way along the narrow staircase between the shop and the law office next door would afford her a more discreet route to the front door.

Norill halted her progress up the steps at the first landing.

Why was the side door to the basement ajar?

She hesitated before extending a gloved hand toward the door. It quietly swung further inward. Her eyes hurriedly scanned the basement entry but to no avail. She'd heard Tekla describe the basement as being laid out like a rat's maze with a host of passages and storage rooms to navigate.

Dare she enter?

"Norill?"

She jumped at the sound of Mr. Erickson's voice from the bottom of the staircase. He was red faced, his sleeves rolled up exposing his forearms, and he bore a worn wrench in one hand and a dirty piece of cloth in another.

"What are you doing out here?" he asked as he wearily began to ascend toward her.

"I … I was … bringing Tekla back her bicycle and …"

"Tekla's not here. Went home some time ago," Mr. Erickson remarked as he dabbed sweat from his forehead. "I've been in the sub-basement working on the boiler. Hades would be cooler than the shop right now and no repairmen are available until tomorrow."

"Oh," Norill intoned.

Erickson cleared his throat.

"Did you open that?" he inquired, motioning toward the door with his wrench.

"No," she shook her head. "Mr. Erickson, would it be

all right if I used the shop's phone? I need to speak to my brother."

It took a few extra seconds for her words to fully register with her employer as his attention remained fixed upon the open door.

"I'd swear I locked that. Yes, but keep it brief," he instructed as they entered the basement.

After making a point to lock the door behind them, Mr. Erickson led them both through the crowded warren to a staircase, which they quickly ascended into the back hallway near his office.

"Everything's all right with your mother I trust?"

The shop was indeed stifling.

"It's complicated," was all she would allow herself to offer as she hastily removed her head scarf and gloves.

"Should I use your office phone or the one at the front counter?" Norill asked.

"Oh, I should think … Good God! My shop!"

They both stared wordlessly at the disaster before them.

"We have to call the police," Mr. Erickson declared as he surveyed the ransacked mess of his business.

Each waded in the opposite direction as they sought a path around numerous obstacles to the front of the bookshop. Norill continued her struggle to reach the front counter as her companion examined the forced front door.

"And you saw no one when you arrived?" he questioned as he inadvertently knocked over a mass of books and swore loudly.

"I came in the same way you did," she quickly reminded him as she flung curls from her left eye and at last reached for the phone.

"The register," he uttered as he staggered toward the overturned device on the floor.

Norill took the opportunity to search for the copy of Ibsen she'd set aside for the commando but failed to locate it anywhere near the counter. But eying the ramshackle condition of the shop, it could still be buried nearly anywhere.

"Blast!" cried Mr. Erickson as he beheld the empty register drawer. "I'd better go check the safe!"

Norill dialed the phone as the man frantically retreated to the back office. At least they wouldn't have to dust anymore.

*

The smell of freshly brewed coffee recalled her to life.

After opening her eyes, Norill lay quietly considering the unfamiliar surroundings. She'd been so exhausted last night that it wasn't until now that she fully realized the unforgiving nature of the mattress; however, the pillows and comforter were exceedingly plush. Groggily, she rose and redressed in her clothing from the previous day before shuffling out into the main room.

Tekla sat at a table looking out the front window, down upon the street. A steaming mug was cupped in her hands. She half turned, obviously sensing Norill's approach more than realizing how close she was.

"Oh, oh, you're up. I figured you'd be sleeping another hour or more. Did I wake you? Oh, I'm so sorry I woke you. After yesterday you should probably sleep for a week. You know I have a friend who claims she slept once for three days. Do you believe that? Three days! Which of course I maintain is simply impossible … coffee?" Tekla finally inquired, noticing her friend's stuporous gaze at the mug in her hands.

Norill slowly nodded before sitting down at the nearby table as Tekla bustled into the kitchen. She returned with an array of breakfast items.

"I couldn't sleep so I cooked," Tekla explained. "Go

ahead, plenty more. I'll go get that coffee. Cream?"

They shared a quiet but pleasant meal.

After such sparse meals the previous day, Tekla's offerings were both a sumptuous and welcome change of pace. Although a part of Norill could not help but feel guilty as she ate. The war rationing made every meal a more cherished event. That Tekla shared her food so freely with her, sincerely touched Norill, to say nothing of the kindness of allowing her to sleep here last night.

"Aren't you having more?" Norill asked the other woman who'd set aside a lone piece of toast.

Tekla took a long sip of her coffee before answering.

"Never been big on breakfast but figured you could use it this morning after last night's troubles. Mr. Erickson phoned a little bit ago. Says the radiator is still broken. He wants us back tomorrow though to start cleaning up. At least they didn't get into the safe. Small miracle there if you ask me."

Norill sighed and nodded but offered no further comment. Tekla pressed on.

"Strange the bookshop being ransacked like that. You'd think someone would have seen something. Thank you so much for bringing my bicycle back last night. Think your mother got settled all right?"

"I'm sure she did," Norill wearily smiled, which seemed to please her friend.

"Good that Mrs. Naess had that spare key of yours," she offered.

Norill's thoughts returned to the strained conversation she'd had over the phone with her brother last night. He'd all but refused to allow their mother to stay with him, even though his lodgings were much bigger than Norill's.

Angry and tired, she'd stopped by Tekla's simply to drop off the bicycle but after the trying conversation with Rejor and a short talk with Vinni about giving the spare key to Norill's rooms to her mother, she'd acceded to Tekla's offer to stay.

"Would you mind if I stayed here for a few days? Just until I can get my mother settled into something more permanent," Norill inquired as she poured herself more coffee.

"Of course," Tekla beamed, reaching out and putting a comforting hand briefly over Norill's.

"Thank you," Norill said softly.

Her gaze grew distant as the myriad of problems she faced preyed upon her mind.

"May I ask you something?" Tekla hesitantly posed.

Norill looked to her and waited.

"I've only met your brother on a few occasions, but he's always been quite affable. Why is he so reticent toward your mother? Surely, you must have told him about the Nazis stealing her home. For God's sake, your family's home."

Norill shook her head, uncertain how much she should share.

"They've been acrimonious for almost as long as I can remember. Rejor was always closer to our father but he blames her for his blindness. First his wife went missing, now the war, and my father's fate have strained their relationship even more. His refusal last night doesn't surprise me, but it does hurt."

"His wife went missing. That's one you've never mentioned before. When did that happen? What was she like? Do the police know?"

Tekla opened her mouth to say more, and then closed it before suddenly standing to clear the dishes.

"I shouldn't have pried," she acknowledged as she worked.

"On the contrary, it feels good to talk to someone about it all," Norill reassured her as she too stood and began to help clean off the table.

Not used to such compliments, Tekla paused before carrying an armload of dishes into the kitchen. Norill could not fail to notice the smile that graced Tekla's face as she did so.

"To be honest, Lisbeth was always a bit of a mystery to me," Norill began. "She was just there one day. They said they met through an article he was working on for his newspaper, before the war, but both of them kept most of the relationship details to themselves. We were never close. They married in secret. Then one day, just before the invasion, she vanished."

"Good heavens," Tekla intoned, clicking her tongue in thought. "And no trace of her since?"

Norill shook her head.

"None I've ever heard of but then again Rejor isn't one to share. Lisbeth was actually closer to Mother than to me, but she rarely talks about her much either. Still …"

"What?" Tekla prompted after a long silence as Norill stared out the window at nothing.

"What?" Norill finally asked, recalling herself.

"Still what?"

Norill's hand shot up to her temple as her head began to throb.

"I'm sorry Tekla. I promise I'll finish cleaning up the dishes but first I need to lie down for a bit."

Without further comment, Norill returned to her room. There she rested in solitude for some time. Images of Lisbeth returned to her mind.

For not the first time the poor woman's fate prayed on her mind. And she knew, her mother was keeping a secret regarding her mysterious disappearance from her daughter. Rejor had repeatedly hinted as much.

What could have transpired between the three of them before Lisbeth's fateful vanishing? Was she still alive? What might have befallen her once the Nazis arrived if she still lived? How could her brother tolerate not knowing?

Much as she was growing to sincerely appreciate the true friendship developing between her and Tekla, she genuinely wondered if they'd ever be able to finish the conversation they'd started about Lisbeth.

And now what of her father? What of her father?

Norill clutched the pillow she held tighter to her chest as the tears began.

**

As she arched her strained back, Norill suddenly heard Mr. Erickson's summons. An exhausted Tekla just nodded as she continued to sort and pour over the multitude of books slowly being assembled into loose piles they could eventually shelve. Norill rose and trekked back to Mr. Erickson's cramped office.

Why did it always smell like vanilla in here?

"Ah, Norill," Mr. Erickson casually noted as she entered.

Without preamble, he proffered an envelope. Norill stared blankly at it.

"For your mother," he said by way of explanation as he hurriedly jotted in a ledger.

When it was not seized from his hand, Mr. Erickson paused, stopped writing, and motioned for Norill to sit in one of the seats opposite the desk he occupied.

"It's money for your mother. Shameful what the Nazis have done to you all," he plainly stated. "It's not much, but we all need to support each other during this damn war. That is how we beat them."

She'd never heard her employer speak so openly and passionately about either the Nazis or the war.

Norill paused, struck by both the unexpected kindness and unique behavior of Mr. Erickson. In all the years that she'd known him, he'd hardly ever strayed beyond subjects related to work. But war changed people. Maybe, so did the recent break-in.

"Thank you," Norill said in humility as she finally took the envelope.

Mr. Erickson seemed to relax a measure, aware that this conversation was a break in his normal demeanor.

"When your mother is ready, my wife would enjoy having you both over for dinner. We have been lax in doing so since your father was called to service."

Norill smiled awkwardly and nodded in gratitude.

"How is your brother these days?" Mr. Erickson asked.

"Well, I suppose," Norill stated, trying to divorce herself from the strained state between her mother and brother. "His affairs keep him quite busy."

Mr. Erickson was quiet as he intently studied her.

"Yes, I can see how his affairs could be quite … taxing. Thank you, Norill. I'll be out shortly to help you and Tekla."

**

Three days after her arrival, Norill was both restless and eager to return more of the kindness Tekla had shown her. Their discussions had grown increasingly more in-depth and welcome. They were truly enjoying each other's company much more than either would have realized before spending such time in close quarters.

Tekla seemed to have lived all over Norway and it was fascinating to hear about her travels and insights. Norill had only ever seen a small portion of her nation, to say nothing of the world. Tekla spoke little of family, being an only child, but could sympathize with Norill's loss of a parent as her mother had died when she was quite young. Her father now lived in Scotland with a new wife and a son, who Tekla had never met.

For her part, Norill did try to talk more about Lisbeth but with so many unknowns the conversations could only turn to either speculation or silence. They talked of both her mother and brother's good and negative qualities and for hopes they dared to dream about when the war was over.

"Do you think you'll ever marry?" Norill asked as they sipped on a shared bottle of mead Tekla had been saving since the start of the occupation.

To her surprise, Tekla didn't engage in her usual chatty response.

"To the right sort, I suppose," was all she offered. "And how about you? Any men in your life?"

"Not the right sort," Norill dryly replied as she examined her glass. "Too many Nazis and not enough Norwegians. Why does it have to be so hard to meet any good ones?"

"What would make a 'good one' for you?" Tekla pressed.

Norill allowed herself to savor a mixture of both dreams and memories as she contemplated the question. Her first kiss. The first time she'd removed her panties for a lover. Meeting someone and just feeling the thrill and excitement of knowing the relationship felt right.

For the present, relationships meant danger.

"I suppose right now, someone who could make me feel safe," she answered. "Cared for, someone who wanted to know me, who could thrill me but respect me."

"Sounds nice," Tekla agreed as she tossed back her glass. "I'd just take someone who's a good lay."

At first Norill was more than a bit shocked by this comment, never having seen this side of Tekla before but soon they were laughing uncontrollably.

The next morning, Norill decided she'd handle the shopping while Tekla put in extra time at the bookshop. She knew of a farm near the edge of town with beehives that might have fresh honey. Maybe they could figure out a way to make their own mead.

She made the usual rounds in the town's modest marketplace and shops. Food and supplies were still at a premium with rationing and dwindling imports, but she'd become savvy enough over the past few years to know when and where to shop to compensate for most shortages. In fact, this skill had become a point of personal pride for her. She might not always adapt gracefully to change but she could always handle shopping come what may.

Her pursuit of honey forced her to bike through several checkpoints to reach the farm. Each presented its own unique encounters. At some, the soldiers were pleasant, professional, and quick. At others, they were belligerent, singled out others to undergo a more rigorous detainment, or unjustly made one feel inferior in their own hometown.

Norill would exchange hasty glances to those who'd been detained as familiar faces would look longingly back at her, their eyes alive with fear, humiliation, or anger but each knew she was helpless to alter whatever fate awaited them. A cursory look from an officer manning the radio was enough warning to her that it was time to move on. Still, the journey was upsetting, and it was with great relief when the final checkpoint was behind her and she was able to reach the farm unmolested.

She filled her basket with as many honey jars that could be safely transported, rested, and talked to the farm owners before starting the long sojourn back. The afternoon was pleasant with a vivid blue sky, playful breeze, and the restful sounds of birds all about her along the wooded lane.

Why couldn't more days be like this?

Her senses drank in the calm.

It was then that she heard a vehicle speeding up behind her. The familiar engine sound left no doubt that this was a German transport, so she was not surprised at the sight of the troop transport truck as it flew by. She was, however, very surprised seconds later when it inexplicitly slowed to a stop and parked along the side of the road ahead of her.

Norill's legs grew light as her heart began to race.

Should she keep going or turn back?

There were no side roads or nearby paths she could easily take. Isolated, she was vulnerable to whatever dark whims these soldiers harbored but to turn and flee up the road presented its own problems.

Her mind returned to the faces she'd witnessed of those detained earlier. The fear and the hopelessness on each. She wondered what fate had befallen each by now.

There was no movement from anyone in the truck as she slowly approached. Her mind and emotions each screamed at her to choose an action before the Nazis did.

Without warning, the back gate of the truck dropped open and the canvas opening was drawn back to reveal at least ten Nazi soldiers inside. Three jumped down, two armed, and began to walk slowly toward Norill, who slammed on the bike's brakes.

She wanted to scream, she wanted to run, but either could result in her being detained or much worse. What did they want? Would anyone hear her scream?

The men stalked closer and closer.

Every nerve in her body cried out for her to run but it was too late.

The armed men took up position on either side of her as the other stepped forward and motioned for her papers. For a horrifying moment, when she reached into her pocket, she feared they'd fallen out. Her sudden frantic movement caused the armed men to instinctively jump, but the man before them motioned them off before they could finish raising their guns.

With a trembling hand, she turned her identity papers

over to the Nazi.

"Norill Haugen," was all he said as he flicked his eyes between the frightened woman and her papers.

She tried to speak, but he waved her off instantly. Instead, he slowly circled the bike, scrutinizing every inch of her body.

Norill fought against her fears.

She knew he was enjoying her helplessness.

Reaching the front of the bike, the man fixed her with his eyes, each sizing up the other. Wordlessly, he retrieved a lone jar from her bicycle basket, unscrewed the lid, and sniffed the contents before tasting a sample.

"*Das ist gut,*" he declared to the others who immediately began helping themselves to her jars of honey.

The man again threateningly held her gaze, but she offered no protest as they stole her gifts for Tekla. Unexpectantly, he removed his right glove, stuck a finger in the jar he held, and withdrew a long liquid strand before reaching out and slowly rubbing the honey onto Norill's lips.

She had never felt so vulnerable and humiliated at once.

Her fingers forcibly clutched the bicycle's handle bars as she fought the urge to strike out at the man violating her as the Nazi soldiers began to laugh.

The corners of her eyes burned with tears.

The soldier moved closer, seemingly ready to lick the honey from her lips. Norill closed her eyes in abject terror as her lungs filled for one final outburst before the violation came.

Her scream was cut off by the sound of a horn blaring from a staff car approaching from town. The soldiers froze in a mixture of puzzlement and annoyance. The car stopped directly opposite of them.

"*Guten tag,*" Gerntz casually announced as he nonchalantly exited the car.

Seeing no officer in the car with him, the soldiers immediately began to protest his obnoxious interruption of their fun, and a short but heated conversation ignited between them all. It moved so rapidly that Norill lost most of it before Gerntz inexplicitly pushed past one of the soldiers and grabbed her off the bike, which landed with a clatter and the sound of shattering glass from the jars as it hit the ground. More shouting erupted between the men and the lead soldier withdrew his pistol.

Rapidly, Gerntz relented and tried a new tactic.

Soon the men were laughing again, all but the lead soldier. Gerntz shrugged as he withdrew his Luger pistol. The soldiers responded as they again started to raise their weapons, but he paid them no mind. Instead, he scanned the nearby trees. He found what he was looking for in a tree growing out of a nearby ravine and loaded a bullet into the chamber.

He roughly grabbed Norill again and hauled her unwillingly in the direction of the tree.

"Shoot that bird," he ordered urgently in Norwegian as soon as they stopped.

"What?"

Gerntz pressed the gun into her hand.

"Shoot the bird!"

Norill looked down at the gun in her hand and then to the bird. She would have looked at Gerntz, but he'd already turned and was walking away from her, pointing, and repeatedly shouting his order.

"Shoot the bird!"

"Shot the bird!!"

Her eyes again dropped to the gun in her hand. Was this a trick?

For a fleeting host of heartbeats, she truly felt the power of what she held. Norill looked longingly at Gerntz's back. She could kill him. She knew it. Soon after joining the resistance, Haktor had insisted on teaching her the basics of firing a gun. It was simple. No, she could kill one of the soldiers. The one who'd humiliated her, who was ready to ....

She could taste the honey still on her lips. How wonderful would it feel to destroy these men, these enemies? Avenge the dead. Avenge her father.

Fate sang in her heart.

Maybe she could even escape before they shot her. The fantasy died, as would she if she raised the gun. She knew it, everything she was begged her to heed reason.

The hardened soldiers waited, primed as the seconds echoed by.

Reluctantly, Norill let the gun clatter to the ground and backed away.

Gerntz stopped shouting and only birdsong shattered the stillness.

If the soldiers were going to kill them, they'd do it now.

The lead soldier unleashed a torrent of curses upon Gerntz as he reprimanded his reckless behavior. Cool under the verbal onslaught, Gerntz pulled him aside and withdrew a paper from his jacket pocket. With some encouragement, the lead soldier read it, shoved it unceremoniously back at Gerntz, and motioned to his men before they all proceeded back to the troop truck. They made sure to destroy any remaining honey jars before leaving.

Neither Norill nor Gerntz said a word as the transport disappeared from sight.

Wordlessly, he grabbed her bike and began loading it on the back of the car. Overwhelmed, Norill sat numbly in the backseat. The silence was only broken after they had arrived back to the bookshop. Just as Norill opened the door, Gerntz finally spoke, without turning to face her.

"I told you not to leave town."

Any protest died on her lips.

Gerntz got out and removed the bicycle from the back of the car. Norill could not meet his eyes as he handed it to her. He left without a word.

When she did look up, it was as if half of the square was watching her. Slowly, she turned and began to walk both her and the bike toward her destination.

During the entire trip, Norill never made eye contact nor spoke to anyone. Only when she was again alone near Tekla's did she breakdown and finally scream.

**

Several days later, as evening became dusk, she was alone in Vinni's house. Haktor was still missing and whatever was bothering Vinni kept her isolated and closed off. Their conversations the last few days were always short and tense, as if she was shielding Norill from something. Still, pretenses needed to be maintained, as did their secret transmitting operations, so the two women coexisted as best they could.

The disquiet between them could not be asserting itself at a worse time.

Gerntz and the Nazis were still lurking, her father was likely dead, Mr. Erickson's shop inexplicably wrecked, her family's property stolen, the mysterious plea for help from the Allied commando, now Vinni, her second mother, was keeping her at bay. It wounded Norill deeply.

Almost as much as her own family did.

Both Rejor and their mother remained distant, but she hoped to see them both tomorrow. She longed to restore some sense of unity among her family and some measure of peace to her life in general.

Norill settled upon the piano bench and for a time absently played a variety of songs. The activity provided the desired effect. Music had always granted her comfort.

Still, it was hard to concentrate.

What was Vinni out doing right now? Where was Haktor? Were more resistance cells in danger? Were they concealing this fact from her for some reason?

She frequently paused her playing, convinced she had heard someone at the door but each time the tranquility of the empty house remained undisturbed. Distracted, her thoughts turned to another mystery.

She'd set her belongings next to the piano when she arrived. Norill now glanced at the front door again before reaching down to retrieve the object of her musings. Tekla had given it to her less than twenty-four hours earlier, but she'd been able to draw few concrete conclusions about its true significance. Its revelation was thanks largely to a casual conversation they'd had after a demanding day of reorganizing the bookshop.

"I almost forgot. You mentioned a man who'd reserved a copy of Ibsen the other day was expected at the store," Tekla had begun, capturing Norill's attention immediately.

"I meant to tell you that a gentleman did come in and pick it up, but one was returned less than an hour later."

"What do you mean one was returned?" Norill questioned.

"Well, the copy that was returned is not a version we sell," Tekla insisted as she walked to retrieve something from a drawer.

"Did you keep it?" Norill asked.

Tekla nodded as she reached into the drawer and retrieved the book.

"And that's not the oddest thing. Mr. Erickson heard me arguing with the man about refunding the money and came over. The two looked at each other, and Mr. Erickson apologized and refunded the money without question. Less than an hour later the radiator broke. When I went into the back to say something to Mr. Erickson about the heat, he was on the phone having a rather terse conversation. He hung up as soon as he saw me and told me that I was finished for the day and should go home. And then there are these markings in the book."

Different pages contained different circled letter and numbers, seemingly at random. Norill had pressed Tekla for a description of the man she'd dealt with, but based on her recollections, it soon became clear that not only were two different books involved, but the transactions had been carried out by two different men. Similar looking to one another but definitely different, just like the copies of the Ibsen book; it was also clear that neither was the same man who'd made contact with her at the café the evening of her brother's birthday.

Since that initial encounter she had seen no further sign of the commando's existence, none save possibly the marked copy of the Ibsen book she held in her hand. There must be a code in use but how was she to decipher it? Maybe Rejor or Haktor (if he ever turned up again) would know.

Her musings were ceased by a hasty knock at the door, which almost immediately began to open. Startled, Norill hurriedly dropped the book back among her belongings crumpled on the floor.

Norill felt her breath seize in her chest as Gerntz stepped inside the house and slowly closed the door. All she was aware of were the striking blue eyes staring into hers.

He soundlessly studied her as Norill fought her urge to flee. If she did, he'd either catch her outright or bring the might of the Nazi occupiers to bear against both her and her family. With so much at stake Norill remained still at the piano, betraying only the faintest of trembles as Gerntz passed within an inch of her as he sought evidence of others in the house. Each heavy tread of his polished boots against the wooden floors sounded like thunder.

Where was Vinni?

Gerntz was approaching her again, apparently satisfied they were alone. Had he followed her here and waited outside until he was all but certain she was alone? Time slowed and the familiar surroundings assumed a surreal quality as first he towered menacingly behind her before leaning down and rifling into her belongings.

Norill tried not to think of the coded book. Was that what he was after?

She kept her eyes fixed on the piano keys, too terrified to look anywhere else. If only she had a weapon.

She heard him stand and seconds later felt the rough skin of his hand on her right shoulder. Norill closed her eyes. She wanted to scream but could sense no utterance would come. Her heart was beating so fast that it felt as if it filled the entirety of her chest.

A lone finger traced across the top of her back as he moved and sat upon the open portion of the bench beside her. Every nerve on the left side of her body seemed to come alive at once. Inches from her now, Norill decided it was finally too much to bear, but when she moved to flee Gerntz grabbed her waist and forced her back down upon the bench.

"Dammit, play something," she heard him order but her mind struggled to make her body respond.

One of his hands released her as he fumbled for something. A sheet of music promptly appeared against the stand above the keyboard.

"Play!"

Without thought her fingers moved into position and seconds later they began striking the keys as dictated by the notations in front of her. Norill's foot worked the pedals.

"You're playing too fast. Slow the tempo," Gerntz instructed.

Norill nodded, grateful for once that her blonde curls now masked a portion of her face. She could not look at him, but she did obey.

This composition was fairly new to her and to her surprise Gerntz kept placing new pages of it on the stand. The longer she played the more his clasp on her loosened until miraculously it was gone.

Norill's breathing became more labored as she reached the more difficult portion of the work, in part because it was intended to be played by two people. Suddenly she saw Gerntz place his fingers in a starting position over the keyboard. They hung there until the notations dictated that he should join.

He played flawlessly, even effortlessly, through the remainder of the piece.

As the dying tones from the last chord struck reverberated in the air, Norill at last looked to Gerntz. He was clearly not a novice musician as he'd claimed. Curiosity now replaced fear as the room again became still.

"I had to be sure," Gerntz began. But though it was the same man, it was not Gerntz's voice she was hearing. Both the language and the accent were different. "Listen to me very carefully. I'm an Allied spy and you are in great danger."

CHAPTER FOUR

A FLAME ONCE LIT

Time could not aid her. Devoid of it, Norill's heart was a living flame, as conflicting thoughts and emotions fought for resolution. The next words she spoke, a shift of her fingers, a fleeting notion read in her eyes could be her final undoing. He would kill her to keep his secret, even if it wasn't true. Gerntz's entire being, from the imploring demand for understanding and fear in his eyes, to his frozen posture, to his roiling spirit burned for her response.

What dare she say?

The words in her mind were daggers, poised and ready to strike. She felt light, dizzy, but formidably resolved. She would know his truth.

Even if it destroyed her.

A subtle, innocuous noise outside rent their wordless commune of shared shock and paranoia. She would attempt to flee. He could see it in the precipitous tension of her muscles. With no choice, Gerntz again seized her. The mission would fail, lives would be lost, including possibly his own, if he allowed her to leave.

Norill's adrenaline fueled strength was formidable. Still, she must listen. The precious seconds fled into nothing.

"You should not be telling me this," Norill chastised as her words accompanied her struggles. "I don't want to know. I don't want to know!"

He tightened his grip to gain her attention and pulled her in close. She sucked in a lusty breath in alarm to which he minutely relaxed his grasp.

She must listen!

"They know who you are," he urgently whispered. "They know about this place's connection to the resistance. Think! Think! How many will you kill if you ignore my warning? Think about all that is at stake for you, your family, your nation. The man from the café …."

Norill's breathing changed, her muscles relaxed to a degree

as she looked downward, twisted her body away from him on the bench, and remained reticent for a time.

"I don't know who you mean."

Gerntz shifted his face away from the mass of her hair that threatened to impede his own breathing. He turned her violently toward him again and their eyes locked. Several heartbeats passed between them before he spoke again.

"They know," he repeated as her tiring efforts to gain freedom finally slackened.

He waited but she offered no more before he continued.

"I saved you from those soldiers on the road. I told my superiors that you're not linked to resistance activities and that I can prove it. I can save you, but you must be truthful with me now or I cannot. Do you understand? Do you UNDERSTAND?" he barked.

"YES!" Norill cried. "Yes, yes, I understand. Yes."

Seconds after they heard the distinct squeal of truck tires outside, he was kissing her. In disarray and confusion, Norill found herself kissing him back as the front door was broken in and a host of Nazi soldiers barged into the house. Several trained rifles on the frozen couple at the piano as others rushed upstairs and about the house, searching.

The raid's commander entered and casually assessed the situation. He met Gerntz's gaze, glanced hastily at Norill but did not address them directly. A soldier's shout soon beckoned him upstairs as others continued to search the lower portion of the residence and kept alert eyes on their prey seated on the piano's bench.

Norill's face blanched as her pulse beat like wings ready to race from her fragile body as the officer disappeared from view. If they'd found the concealed door and gone into the attic where the radio equipment was ....

A host of heavy boot steps quickly descended the stairs as the commander and his soldiers returned. One carried a fuel container and disappeared out the front door immediately. Another soldier stayed by his superior's side.

Norill felt diminutive, exposed under the men's intense gazes. But it was not their faces, rather, the weapons they carried that held her complete attention. When the commander did speak, at first, it was as if she was hearing his words across a great distance.

"Fraternizing with the locals, Gerntz. And I had such high hopes for you," the officer admonished. "Tell me, either of you, where is Vinni Naess?"

Norill and Gerntz exchanged a fleeting, uncomfortable look before he responded.

"We have not seen her tonight."

The officer smiled.

"Shame. Still, a blind woman shouldn't be too hard to find," he noted, bidding them to rise as he ceremoniously donned his gloves.

"Shall we?" he asked politely, nodding toward the front door.

As they stood, Norill wondered if there was any way to dispose of the potentially incriminating Ibsen book in her bag, but it clung to her like a lead weight. Too many eyes watched.

As they stumbled outside the bright lights on the assembled Nazi trucks momentarily blinded her. Gerntz, however, adjusted faster and helped her down the remaining stairs.

Upon walking around one of the trucks, another sense (this time smell) of Norill's was assaulted before the horror of what she was seeing was fully realized. She gasped before covering her mouth and nose as she retreated several steps back against Gerntz, who also recoiled in horrified surprise.

The commander paused and looked down at the smoldering remains of a man, who'd been burnt nearly beyond recognition.

"Can you explain the half-empty fuel canister found in the house?" he inquired as he stood above the smoldering remains. "I'm sure it would hasten our investigation."

Norill frantically shook her head, while Gerntz simply replied, "*Nein.*"

As a car pulled up behind the commander, Norill stole a glance to see if she could identify the immolated remains, but the dread that filled her after Nazi officer's next sentence arrested her efforts.

"Perhaps your memories will improve at headquarters."

Norill lowered her head and closed her eyes.

She was going to die.

***

On the fourth day of detention, they came for her again. She was brought from the cell to the same dimly lit room she'd been questioned in for countless hours days earlier. Wordlessly, she assumed the chair across from the smoking Nazi officer, who at least was not grinning at her this time. By design, her lack of sleep, harsh treatment, and a poor diet made Norill feel unequal to enduring another prolonged round of questioning by the petty man before her.

If only she could sleep.

"Name," her opposite needlessly barked.

"Norill Haugen," she mechanically responded without looking at the Nazi interrogator.

How would he play the encounter this time, she dully wondered?

The officer paused, analyzing her, before closing the folder he'd been consulting, placing it on the table then covered it with folded palms. He stoically waited, mirroring his averse companion's feigned disinterest.

He had time.

Norill made no attempt to address him, unwilling to play this twisted power game. If he had more questions, eventually, he would ask. She kept her eyes downcast, absently exploring the pattern of shadows upon the floor.

A shattering impact upon the back of Norill's head sent her lurching forward.

She instantly tasted blood seconds after her face struck the metal table. For a time, all she saw were alternating flashes of light; all she knew was the searing pain emanating from the back of her skull. When her vision cleared at last, the Nazi across from her was again smiling.

She repressed her anger. Norill refused to give him the satisfaction.

"I have … nothing more … to add to my statement," she managed, steeling herself to be struck again from behind by the butt of the guard's gun.

The officer casually raised a hand to restrain the second blow before it could be delivered. Norill offered a silent prayer as she struggled to breathe normally. The Nazi paused to slowly retrieve and light another cigarette before again opening the folder and resuming his review the documents inside. She'd never been so consumed with feelings of pure loathing for another.

How could anyone be so dispassionately inhuman?

The monster stirred.

"You will not leave here until you give me something useful, such as the truth," he evenly informed her without taking his eyes off the folder's contents as he took a deep, indifferent inhalation of his cigarette.

Norill inwardly struggled against the dark, very real fears, living in her soul, while fighting to maintain a neutral expression toward her tormentor.

"Now, you still claim not to know any of these men?" he asked as he slapped eight, by now all too familiar, photos down on the table before her.

The frozen faces again stared blankly back at her. Norill's eyes itched, her shoulders were knots. Most of the men were dressed in nondescript clothing, however, one was dressed in a British Royal Air Force officer's uniform.

Why did they keep asking her this?

Hour after hour they'd asked almost no questions about Gerntz, Vinni, the bookstore, her mother; and yet, they seemed fanatical about her recognizing one of these men's faces. Several times now she'd considered making up some false statement about one of them just to see what they did. But that would be careless and foolish.

Her eyes darted briefly to the officer. Couldn't this idiotic man tell she had nothing to offer?

Perhaps she should just give up Gerntz.

He was probably lying to her and then at least she'd be rid of him for good. But, if he was telling the truth, what dangers might she expose others to and what answers to the endless questions that plagued her mind would be lost?

Her resolve stiffened as she realized she wanted those answers. Unfortunately, for Norill, her heartless interrogator perceived her emotional shift as well.

"Bring us some water," the Nazi officer coldly ordered. "It appears we will be here for some time."

***

Where was she?

Norill awoke in a state of abject confusion. The bedroom she discovered herself in was relatively dark, expensively adorned, and wholly unfamiliar. No, no something about the room did hold ghostly, long-dormant memories for her. The din of muted, lively conversations below captured her wavering attention before she again sank into unconsciousness.

When she struggled to consciousness once more there was no longer any need to consider her surroundings. She knew, and the revelation did not comfort her as her gaze fell upon the room's other occupant.

"How's your head?" Sigdis delicately questioned, as Norill fought to regain full alertness.

"I'm in your home?" she asked, more to stall for time than to confirm information she already knew from the woman perched on a chair beside her bed.

They'd been mere children the last time Norill had been here for a grade school sleepover with all their friends during some long-forgotten weekend. The only fixed memory Norill possessed from that experience was how much more she loved the pancakes served in the tavern below the next morning than the ones at home.

"You remember," Sigdis smiled in obvious relief, though if it were for the fact that Norill's memory was intact or for some measure of grace visited upon herself, Norill could not tell.

Her former friend looked thinner and more despondent than Norill could ever remember seeing her.

"Why am I here?" Norill hurriedly queried as she attempted to sit up.

The motion made her head spin as her vision fragmented and nausea seized her. After several endless heartbeats, the sensation mercifully subsided, allowing her to lower her head back to the pillow. She moaned slightly as the nerves settled back down.

Sigdis got some water and helped her drink it before responding.

"They were rather rough with you in detention. You've been here two days. Tekla and your mother argued for your release before they came to me to try to get you out. I suppose after Vinni's arrest ..."

"What!" Norill ignored the spinning this time as she sat bolt upright. "Vinni's been arrested! We've got to get her out!"

Norill's spirit cried for action but her body refused as Sigdis gently eased her back down. Norill's eyes couldn't help but be drawn to the Nazi party pin affixed to Sigdis' dress. Did she wear that by choice or could it be as she'd once told Norill, she had never truly given in to her family's stern and unwavering support of their occupiers?

She wanted to feel true pity for her former friend, but this was war and, reluctantly or otherwise, they'd each chosen a side. God help whoever had chosen wrong.

"I don't know anything more than that she was taken a day or two after you were arrested. They seem to be convinced she has something to do with the man they found burned in the street. Can you imagine? Vinni, of all people, they think murdered someone," Sigdis scoffed.

"What about the dead man?" Norill soberly inquired. "Do they know who it was?"

Sigdis looked away, haunted.

"No," she simply said. "Rumors abound but they aren't saying anything definitive. Oh, I hate this war. It's brutal, sick. It twists us all into people we'd rather not be."

A lone tear adorned her cheek as she spoke, as she fought to conceal her own pain.

"Or who we chose to be," Norill challenged offering her no quarter.

For a short time, a deep silence descended upon them, as did voiceless tears, personal demons, and black memories.

"Or who we chose to be," Sigdis' soft voice repeated Norill's last words in a troubled whisper.

"Why did they release me? Why did they release me to you?" Norill demanded, her head starting to hurt again.

"They trust me," Sigdis replied at last lifting her head to

face Norill. “They don’t trust you, Tekla, or your mother. So, they released you to me. That’s all I know. You were obviously abused in there. I’m not heartless. I have no illusions what goes on in the detention center. What type of fate Vinni may be facing at their hands? She is my friend too, Norill.”

Another awkward silence fell between them.

“Thank you,” Norill finally said, placing a hand atop Sigdis’ closest one. “You didn’t have to do this, and I’m not sure how much more I could have taken in there. “

Their eyes met.

“Thank you.”

Their present realities fell away as all the terrible events that had torn them apart vanished, and they were simply two old childhood friends who fortune, and the sundry events of a world filled with alternating beautiful and violent moments, had separated.

Norill had more questions but for now her body needed rest she could no longer fight. She effortlessly lapsed into sleep as Sigdis withdrew her hand.

***

For the next few days, Norill rested fitfully as her body recovered and a host of questions coalesced. She worried that news about her family did not come even though every time she saw Sigdis, she begged her to contact them. For her part, Sigdis appeared and disappeared over the hours and each time she left, Norill agonized about which questions might be safe to try to ask her when she returned.

Had Vinni met her fate? What of Haktor or the mysterious man from the café? How did her mother fit into all this? Why had they shown her those faces in the photos endlessly? Why had she been granted mercy and released from captivity? Which poor soul had lain burnt in the street that night?

What had become of Gerntz? Had Tekla managed to clean up the entire ruined bookstore herself?

In the end, she decided it was too risky to press Sigdis for information. Besides, despite their shared moment, in her heart and to her sorrow, Norill knew it was simply too dangerous to trust her.

Late into the afternoon of the fourth day of her prolonged recovery, Norill decided it was time to leave. Once informed, Sigdis benevolently returned Norill's clothing and items that had been confiscated at the time of her arrest. To her dread, she quickly discovered that the Ibsen book was no longer in her bag.

Her mind and fears instantly tumbled into panic.

Had Sigdis taken it? Could the Nazis have uncovered the secrets it held prompting her sudden release? If so, why let her go at all?

Her thoughts involuntarily summoned the sensations she'd felt during her experience of nearly drowning during childhood again. Norill's muscles seized, her breath fought to escape, and the thundering of her pulse pounded relentlessly in her head as a lurking host of dark potential realities played upon her soul.

Her father was not here to save her this time.

Was all this but a cruel trick that would ultimately see her return to prison before suffering untold torment and death?

Sigdis knocked softly before entering. Norill could tell her attempt to conceal her fears had not been completely successful by the look on Sigdis' face.

"Are you all right? Are you sure you're ready to leave?" she asked.

Norill shook her head in the affirmative, but she felt shaky.

"You're welcome to stay. In fact, would you like to join us for dinner? My parents would so enjoy a short visit?" Sigdis prompted, looking anxious.

Norill wanted to leave but with her head swimming she knew her eventual exit would be slow, to say nothing of where she would go after. Perhaps a brief pause and a few spoonsful of something would revive her. She hesitated a moment longer before agreeing.

Sigdis beamed. "Wonderful, I'll tell them to set an extra place at the table. Just come down when you're ready."

*

An hour later, a cautious Norill gingerly descended from the third floor to the living quarters on the second. It appeared she was not the only guest Sigdis' family was hosting this evening Norill noted as the soft sounds of clinking porcelain, cutlery, and glassware blended with murmuring conversations taking place in the dining room.

She halted her steps, a grim sensation landing hard in her stomach. Maybe it was better just to leave and to send a note of gratitude later. This didn't feel right.

But then again, when was the last time anything had?

Norill seemed to be trapped with few clear allies in what her father called, the Web of Wyrd. She was beholden to a journey of fate, although to where these dark days were ultimately leading her, Norill could not possibly fathom. She was meant to play a role in the drama encompassing her life and those she loved. But would her choices free them or destroy them? Did they matter at all in the Web of Wyrd?

She took a deep breath.

Perhaps this unexpected gathering would provide her with some answers, or at least, a path forward. When she reached the entry to the dining room, she froze, a lamb to the slaughter, surrounded by wolves.

How could she have been so foolish?

Norill felt naked as a fragile newborn as a multitude of judgmental eyes began to slowly turn their attention upon her. Enemy eyes.

"Ah, our final guest has joined us," Sigdis' father announced to those assembled after catching Norill's apprehensive gaze from the head of the table. She read in his visage a perverse pleasure that was quickly hidden from his hawkish features.

A host of Nazi officers accompanied by their wives, lovers, or mistresses now collectively paused in the partaking of their elegant meal to stare back at the young woman with blonde curly hair now framed in the doorway. For an eternity no one moved or spoke as they relentlessly scrutinized everything about this haggard looking interloper.

Norill's eyes traversed the lavish spread set upon the table. Such a sumptuous feast was unimaginable during a time of such lack and shortage. And yet, here it was before her. And she was a mere mortal, cast among a vicious pack of predators, who would see her nation and all like it vanish from the face of the Earth.

When there was nothing left to devour how would they turn upon themselves?

Sigdis, seated near her parents, awkwardly stood, and walked to Norill, each step seeming to echo on the tiled floor. She said nothing as she guided her to a seat, which the young Nazi officer seated next to Sigdis obediently stood and pulled out for Norill. By appearances, he appeared to be Sigdis' paramour, but appearances in this situation were certainly not to be trusted.

"How are you feeling, Norill?" Sigdis' mother asked, at last ending the purgatory.

"Fine," Norill breathed. "Much better. Thank you, I'm most gracious for your hospitality," she managed a halting smile before taking a long sip of water.

“Nonsense,” Sigdis father exclaimed. “After your family’s generous gift to the Fatherland, caring for you in an hour of need is the least we can do.”

“Our gift?” Norill questioned in puzzlement as she set her glass back down.

Her head was splitting again.

“The land, your parents’ farm, of course,” one of the Nazi officers answered, inserting himself into the conversation. “No doubt it will feed our soldiers and cause for some time to come. The contribution of such a rich estate in timber and other natural resources and your loyalty to the Reich should not be overlooked.”

He stood and raised his wine glass to Norill. In short order, the rest of the gathering joined him and waited while, unbidden, Norill’s wine glass was filled.

She’d never felt so humiliated.

First, they steal her land making her mother homeless, murder or imprison her father, torture her, lock up Vinni, and now put on a false show of mocking praise?

It was beyond revolting.

“A toast to you and your family. May such friendships forge a new path for Norway and the Third Reich,” the officer pronounced to a celebratory crowd. The charade was only complete when they all raised their glasses in praise of their twisted master, “Heil Hitler!”

“You’re not drinking?” he asked Norill as the others began to sit back down.

For her part, Norill had made no attempt to join the insulting toast. She was about to explain that in her current condition alcohol wouldn’t help when several men rushed into the room. One held an urgent, harried conference in German with the officer who’d given the toast. The other Nazis nearby could tell immediately that the festivities were ended and began to down drinks, fetch a last bite from their plate, or stand and make apologies to those around them.

They shook Sigdis' father's hand and bade the remaining women a pleasant evening before hurrying out of sight. Seizing the opportunity, Norill turned to Sigdis, offered a final nod of gratitude, and fled from the odious gathering.

*

Norill circled the block a second time, attempting again to ascertain if she was being followed. The darkness, and her recent abusive treatment, emboldened her as she ducked into the narrow alley behind Vinni's house. After two turns and an odd number of paces, she stooped and allowed her fingers to wander among the lower bricks of the house until she found the loose stone she sought.

It gave.

Once retrieved, the formerly hidden key became a reassuring presence in her hand. If all of this were some grand trap, it was better that she spring it now, rather than wait for it to engulf her and those she loved. For all she knew, her family had still not been informed of her release. Better to take such risks now than expose them to reprisals later.

The night air was rich with humidity, and her hot breath fogged up the glass of Vinni's back door as she inserted the key in the lock. Fate, she reminded herself as the spring inside the lock issued a dull ping when she turned the key. Or was it now a path of faith she walked? With a few final stolen glances outside, she entered the confines of the familiar house and locked the door behind her.

For a few minutes, she stood stock still and simply listened.

The house was silent, even the clocks must have run down. Norill dare not turn on a light or betray her presence to anyone watching. She moved slow and got low to the ground when near a window.

The damp air tasted stale, and there was no evidence that Vinni, or anyone else, had been present here for quite some time. After conducting a futile search near the piano for her missing Ibsen book, Norill proceeded upstairs. The stress of crawling and of simply being in Vinni's house after all that had happened was doing her head no favors, but she pressed on.

Reaching her destination, Norill again paused and listened for telltale signs that another horde of Nazi soldiers were about to descend on her, but all was quiet. The only sound was the deafening beat of her pulse in her head. Inwardly, she began to hum notes to old favorites she enjoyed playing on the piano to calm herself.

The effort was only partially successful as she slid through the secret door and ascended to the pitch-black cubby hole that housed their resistance cell's radio equipment. A mixture of horror, relief, and unwelcome musings flooded her as she felt about and realized that the space was bare. Everything resistance-related was gone, including the vital radio equipment.

But why, by whom, and how had this come to be? Haktor, Vinni, the Nazis, Sigdis, Gerntz?

She sneezed violently making her head even more dizzy. She vainly attempted to scan the ensconced space. With nothing more to be learned, Norill sighed in pain and began to retrace her awkward path to escape the house.

"Where are you, Vinni?" she wondered aloud of her friend and mentor. More importantly, would she ever see her alive again?

*

Norill knocked loudly a third time.

She was so tired, and the hour was lost to her. All she longed for was to rest in her own rooms. Outside it had begun to rain, mere seconds after she'd been able to duck inside the building where her rooms were located.

She'd given her mother her keys when she'd moved in after being evicted from the farm. Norill internally berated herself. She'd had two years to make more spare keys, but right now the only set was with Rejor on the far side of town. She paused and considered seeking out her brother. Perhaps, he could answer some of her most vexing questions. But further consideration arrested the thought.

She needed sleep.

At last the sound she'd longed for was issued as her mother finally answered her summons by turning the lock. The door haltingly opened a measure, the chain still in place.

"Mother," Norill breathed in relief, a too long absent smile reaching her lips.

Her mother's face was cloaked mostly in shadow. She made no motions toward her child.

"Mother ...?" Norill's smile faltered. "Mother, I'm exhausted. Open the door, please."

The sound of rain filled the void, but her mother still made no move to unchain the door.

"So, you were released," the older woman finally said in an even tone. "I trust you are well."

Norill was aghast.

How could she even think to make such an assertion?

After all she had endured, it nearly wounded her beyond words.

"No, no Mother. I'm quite far from well," the woman's daughter bitterly responded in a harsh, whispered tone.

For a long moment, they held each other's eye.

"Very well," her mother began. "We'll talk in the morning. I'll call Tekla and let her know you're on your way."

"Mother!" Norill almost stomped her foot in tandem with the word but was restrained by her stunned sense of disbelief.

The older woman paused several seconds before leaning aside the door, retrieving an umbrella, and holding it out through the narrow gap in the doorway. By now, Norill was fuming. She angrily swatted the umbrella down, but her mother only nudged it out into the hallway with her foot before closing and locking the door behind her.

Breathing heavily, Norill pounded on the door several more times and shouted her mother's name but to no avail. Others in the building were clearly stirring behind their closed doors as muttered and shouted curses assailed her. Finally, with no recourse, Norill stooped and picked up the umbrella.

The rain never stopped falling as she journeyed through the bleak night.

**

"Why didn't you wake me up?" Norill sleepily asked, brushing her hair back with her hands as she entered the room.

Rejor looked up from his braille text.

"Well, good evening to you too. For the record, I did try twice to wake you up today. Seems you needed the rest. How's your head?"

Norill sunk into the other end of the sofa. Normally, she would hate losing a day to sleep, but this time it was definitely a blessing. Every part of her body hurt.

"Aches. But it does feel better. Did Tekla or Mother call?"

There was only the briefest unnatural pause.

"I called Tekla and told her you wouldn't be at work today," Rejor said. "I think there are still sausages in the ice box if you're hungry. Oh, I'm afraid I still can't find that spare key to your rooms. I'll keep looking though," he casually mentioned, temporarily returning his attention to his book.

"But nothing from our mother?" Norill warily persisted.

Her brother's face grew dark.

"I've told you for years, she's heartless," Rejor angrily asserted. "And don't tell me again that she made a choice. I suffer every day because of her choice."

No matter how upset she was with her mother, Norill knew they had to speak. Their family was already so fragile, and if Rejor was bringing up his suffering, then he wanted to talk about it. He rarely did.

"As does she," Norill quietly countered. "She has to live with what happened to you and to Asta. We all do."

Rejor banged on the coffee table in front of them. Norill hated when his fierce temper came out.

"She chose Asta. I was supposed to be the one who died, remember. Me! She chose me, her only son to die. She's always seen me as weak. Always interfered with my affairs. Even left you last night out on the streets. How can she be anything but heartless?" Rejor icily asserted.

Norill knew her brother couldn't see her, but she still kept her eyes downcast.

Her mother's actions last night had hurt but Norill knew she loved her children, despite such actions. She understood her brother's rage, but too often he ignored the pain they collectively suffered as a family in favor of embracing his own.

His life had been difficult, there was no denying it. If only there'd been enough medicine that winter. How different their lives would now be.

But there hadn't been enough, and Asta was merely an infant when stricken with the fever. It was only shortly later that the older Rejor was likewise infected.

Norill could still hear Asta's cries in her most nightmarish memories. Their father had been away on business. Her mother tried everything she could to obtain more medicine to fight the fevers, but too many others in town were similarly afflicted and the winter was unusually harsh, making travel difficult. Supplies were short, as was time.

Faced with the possibility of losing two of her children, Norill's mother had been cursed with the choice of how to best use the scant supply of medicine in her possession. Ultimately, she chose to give it all to Asta.

But it could not save the poor infant and she died. Rejor turned out to be the miracle. He lived, but the prolonged high fever permanently took his sight and instilled in him a deep and lasting bitterness toward their mother.

"Father didn't think so," Norill softly reminded her brother. "He chose compassion when he returned and learned of that horrific decision she faced."

Had fate chosen differently, it could just as well be Norill who sat here blind if she'd succumbed to the same illness that had beset her poor siblings. Would their mother really have chosen any differently?

"You always take their side in this," her brother indignantly shook his head but anything else he was about to say died on his lips. He knew it was futile. His rage ebbed.

This was an old argument. One they both knew they were helpless to change the outcome of for Rejor would still be blind and Asta still gone when the argument was over. Nevertheless, he snatched his hand away when Norill offered hers in comfort.

They both sat in lengthy, stony silence.

"We're family," Norill simply affirmed before continuing. "I need to know what's been happening while I was in detention. Where's Vinni? Haktor? Whose body was that in the street that night? What's happened to Gertnz?"

This final question seemed to return Rejor fully back to the present.

"Mother probably thinks you're a spy. A spy for them," her brother posited as he delicately maneuvered a pair of sunglasses, he retrieved from the coffee table, onto his face.

Norill couldn't help but notice that he looked older with them on.

"Me? A spy for the Nazis?" she retorted.

"Half the town already thinks so, why shouldn't Mother?" her brother evenly asserted.

Norill froze, unable to make the words make sense in her mind. After an uncounted host of heartbeats, she regained a measure of composure.

"Why would they think I'm a spy for them? Anyone loyal knows I'm in the resistance," she insisted.

Rejor turned to face her. The coolness of her brother's voice struck Norill.

"Our family farm mysteriously seized. Later you're caught alone in a resistance location with a Nazi officer. The burnt body outside, Haktor apparently gone, Vinni in detention for questioning. Your cell is gone, Norill. And Sigdis …," he paused. "Sigdis taking you into her family home, a den of Nazi sympathizers, out of what … the kindness of her heart?"

Norill wanted to defend herself. To refute any suggestion that she could be involved with the Nazis, but Rejor was right. Objectively, there was genuine room for doubt.

And that was all that was needed to destroy her.

"They rough you up a little. We take you back into our confidence and then …," he trailed off as he reached down to retrieve his fallen book.

"More resistance cells fall." Norill finished the thought.

Rejor solemnly nodded as he stood.

"I'm afraid you can no longer be trusted. It might have been better for you if you weren't released," he callously added.

Norill's heart swelled. How quickly her life seemed a mere shadow of what it had been only a tiny march of days ago.

"Tekla is willing to let you stay with her for a time. Do you want those sausages before you leave?"

**

"Dear heavens! Norill! Oh, Norill, Norill," Tekla practically threw herself upon her friend. "You're safe. I thought you were coming to my place last night. Dear God, it's good to see you," she drew back to study Norill's face. The bruises and cuts were largely healed but even Tekla could tell she'd been through a hell.

She hugged her again, a bit more gently this time, before finally releasing Norill, who, before they parted, returned the warm embrace. At least one person still believed in her and their relationship. There was so much she wanted to say to her mousey but spirited friend; however, overcome by emotion, Norill simply smiled awkwardly and nodded in humble gratitude.

She hadn't been able to bring herself to go to Tekla's last night, lest she suffer a third betrayal. Instead, she'd snuck back into Vinni's still vacant home, careful to rise and be well away before dawn.

With nowhere else to go, she'd used her set of keys to gain early entry to the bookshop, which appeared largely repaired after the recent unexplained vandalism prior to her arrest. Given everything else happening the incident could hardly be dismissed as coincidence, but the reason behind the invasion remained elusive.

Her eyes roved over the familiar setting, engendering an unexpected sense of warmth within her. She'd never felt more grateful to see such an ordinary sight. Flashes of the dark days she'd spent incarcerated threatened to return.

She fixed her mind on the present.

"It's good to see you, Tekla," Norill wearily grinned. "I

see you and Mr. Erickson got the shop back together. What? What is it? What's wrong?"

A complex look of concern graced Tekla's face as she weighed what to say.

"I cleaned it up. By myself. Mr. Erickson has been missing for some time."

"What!" Norill couldn't control her outburst. "When did he go missing?"

Tekla breathed heavily.

"Well, that's just the thing. No one's quite sure. Before the vandalism, he'd been scheduled to go south on a buying trip, remember, and quite honestly that's where I thought he'd gone. Seemed a bit strange that he wouldn't leave a note or call, but with everything going on, I figured he'd told you. But then you were arrested, and he didn't return. I was able to find his itinerary in his office. When I called the numbers of the shops he was due to visit, they all confirmed that he never arrived."

Norill barely had an instant to ruminate before the front door beside them slowly opened, drawing their mutual attention to the familiar, and unwelcome, figure framed in the entry.

"Ah, you're both in. Good. How are we this morning, ladies?" Sigdis inquired as casually as if they'd all just been discussing the weather. Neither Norill nor Tekla paid her much mind as both were transfixed by the armed Nazi soldier stationed behind her.

"What is this?" Tekla harshly demanded. "What's he doing here?"

Sigdis ignored her completely and walked over to take up Norill's hand in a comforting gesture.

"I'm afraid I'm here as a bearer of bad news. Is there someplace private we could sit down?"

Already feeling qualmish in Sigdis' presence, Norill reflexively settled into the nearest chair. She couldn't bring herself to meet Sigdis' eye as the other woman knelt before her. All she could bring herself to focus on were the Nazi sympathizer's shiny, red painted nails.

"Norill. Norill, there's no easy way to say this and I'm sorry I must, but you need to know. Your brother is dead."

There were no words she could summon.

Norill's heart shattered.

Sigdis leaned in closer to whisper in her ear.

"And Gerntz has escaped. You have my word; he will be found."

**

There was no sense of time.

What followed was a series of events that Norill barely processed: crying, people talking to her, questions by more Nazis regarding her whereabouts since leaving Sigdis' home, the morgue, and now, somehow, here with her mother.

They held each other, as if swimmers fighting an undertow so strong, they knew that their parting would mean their deaths.

"You've seen his body?" her mother finally asked. "He was murdered?"

Norill struggled to speak; she could not bring herself to address the second terrible question.

"Briefly," she nodded. "It was him."

"And you're certain that property document bore your father's signature?"

Norill could only nod as the release came.

They wept.

"You're all I have left," her mother finally said as she lovingly stroked her daughter's hair before kissing the top of her head, as she had once done when Norill was a child.

"Your father, your brother … your sister. Only you, my angel."

Norill could feel her mother's tears as they wound trails down her hair to touch her skin.

"I love you," Norill whispered as their embrace and their grief only deepened.

**

It felt like she was coming out of a trance.

"Miss?" the man on the opposite side of the bookstore's sales counter repeated.

Norill brushed back her hair and blinked rapidly as she tore her attention away from the wisps of steam still rising off the teacup on the counter.

How long had he been standing there?

"Yes, yes, sorry. I was just …," she asserted. "How can I help?"

Such an odd idea – help. Norill wasn't even sure if being at home with her mother or trying to feel normal here at work was worse right now. She struggled to remain in the moment.

"Funny you should put it that way, Miss. I was going to ask the same of you," the man explained. "Tell me, do you recognize me?"

The question at least gave her something concrete to focus upon. Norill hastily studied him. The clergyman did seem familiar but only in the vaguest terms.

"We've only met briefly. You meditated in my church for several hours the day your family's property was gifted to the Fatherland," he said by way of enlightenment.

Norill blinked.

"Yes, yes. Of course. The chapel out … yes. What can I do for you?"

"To be honest, I've learned of your family's recent loss

and wondered if you might bless me with your company for an hour or so? I can help you make final arrangements, or if you like, offer spiritual council for Rejor's passing. In fact, I believe we each have something we can offer the other?"

Norill was unmoved. What was this man's game?

The significance of her standoffish demeanor was not lost on the holy man. His opportunity was closing. He cast a harried glance around himself before continuing.

"I believe I may be able to provide answers you cannot find elsewhere," the holy man intoned as he laid a wrapped package down on the counter. "I am at your disposal should you wish it," he concluded with a faint smile and tip of his hat before leaving.

She stared down at what was obviously a concealed book. Uncertain, Norill chose not to call out to Tekla to replace her at the counter. Rather, she quietly rose and locked the front door, recalling to turn the sign on the door to "Closed" before pulling the shade down.

Returning to the counter, Norill quickly tore open the wrapping.

It was a copy of Ibsen's *The Vikings of Helgeland.* In abandon, she rifled through its pages but could only locate a single marked quote. She inaudibly mouthed the words as she read them.

"'Cage an eagle and it will bite at the wires, be they of iron or gold.'"

She closed the book as a tight knot settled into her stomach. This coded message could mean only one thing. The Allied commandos who'd reached out to her weeks ago were still alive!

*

Only the fifth café she visited that evening would serve her.

The others refused.

Rejor had been right. Everyone had lost faith in her. And Sigdis, always ready to play her part, being the one to bring her news of her brother's death only strengthened misconceptions further.

She rested her temples against her upraised hands.

So many deaths and disappearances. So much rapid change. Norill was now all but bereft of real allegiances. Only Tekla, and perhaps her mother remained; the rest were gone.

Dark musings pondered the mysterious fates of Hektor and Vinni. It felt many lifetimes since they'd all been safely together, fighting for a cause greater than any of them. Almost daily now, Norill had thought of reaching out to Sigdis to see if she could learn anything of Vinni's fate but, intuitively, Norill knew such an action could only summon more pain and disaster. She was alone in this.

Lives depended on her making the right choices.

Her fingers unconsciously stretched across her forehead as the enormity of what lay before her seized her mind. A woman who couldn't even get seated for dinner was supposed to be a savior. How could she hope to solve the mysteries surrounding her, much less arrange the rescue of hidden Allied troops? She couldn't even leave town without being arrested. If the situation wasn't so dire, it would be impossible not to laugh out loud.

"May we join you?"

The familiar voice caught her by surprise, which was made even more so seconds later when she raised her head and discovered not just her mother but Tekla standing beside her.

Unbidden, they sat and began to earnestly peruse their respective menus.

For several minutes no one spoke. Norill unconsciously

shifted, uncertain why their presence was making her uncomfortable.

"We only have an hour before curfew," her mother flatly noted, her face largely concealed by the menu she held. Still, the look in her eyes only made her daughter's sense of unease grow.

"Mother, what's happening?"

The women put down their menus in unison as Tekla waved off an approaching server.

"Let's go for a walk," she suggested.

They rose and walked along the waterfront as dusk began to awaken the evening to come. Norill couldn't help but notice their chosen path took them further and further from both the town proper as well as all their living quarters. The path turned, and they passed into a secluded wooded area near the edge of a park where her mother rounded suddenly on her daughter.

"The Nazis are refusing to allow your brother a proper burial. It seems even in death his handicap makes him unworthy of honor. He has already been cremated and scattered," she announced without preamble.

"What?" Norill was aghast but her anguish deepened seconds later.

"That burnt body has also been identified," Tekla quietly added. "It's Mr. Erickson."

Norill wanted to break down again but fought against the urge to do so.

"Why are you telling me this here," she demanded, adding harshly. "Why?"

The other women exchanged a somber glance.

"We know you have not been honest with us," her mother said, returning her full attention to her ill-fated daughter.

"And that lack of honesty endangers us all," Tekla evenly stated. "The entirety of the resistance. Do you now work for the Nazis? Did they break you in there?"

The successive accusations hung in the air. The familiar faces before her might as well have been those of complete strangers in the surreal moment.

So, the final betrayal had come.

"Honesty?" Norill scoffed, finally finding her voice. "How long have I been trying to get you to tell me the truth about the Allied glider the Nazis claim is on your property, Mother?"

"It's not my property anymore," the older woman coolly reminded her. "It belongs to the Fatherland now."

"And I suppose that's my fault too?"

The attack never wavered.

"Was your brother in the resistance? Is that why he's dead?" her mother continued to press.

Norill looked to her friend. No, not friend.

Why wasn't Tekla defending her?

Norill's unspoken pleas found no comfort in the gazes of the others. They would have their answers.

Her heart smoldered.

"Dear God, do you really think I'd betray him? Think that I could …? Especially after what you did? You know what we did the last evening I saw him? We argued. About you! I am always defending your actions to him, always trying to save our family. And for what? For you to turn on me when I need you the most? I've never been more frightened in my life. I can't explain his death any more than I can Mr. Erickson's or of Vinni, or Haktor, or father's fate. I don't know why the Nazis have singled me out to destroy, but they have. And I wish to God they'd either finish the job or arrest me for good because I can't live like this. Watching everyone around me betray me, die, or disappear. I can't live like this."

Her unmitigated pain and sorrow found voice in the grief-stricken tears now running freely down her cheeks. She sunk against her mother's legs, wordlessly begging with her very soul for understanding.

Her mother offered no solace in return.

"Gerntz?" the older woman harshly demanded.

"He's nothing to me. Part of the trap they've ensnared me in. He's escaped. I don't know. Sigdis said he escaped, when she told me about Rejor. He claimed to be a double agent the night we were arrested. I haven't seen him since," she just wanted to close her eyes and have everything as it had once been.

The image of her father's face, strong, loving, and certain, swam momentarily before her.

Was this fate?

"What did Sigdis tell you when you were released from detention?" Tekla softly asked, a small degree of pity in her voice.

Norill fought to remember. It all seemed so long ago.

She pounced on the answer when it came.

"That you'd both been petitioning for my release. But she never reached out to you to let you know I'd been released? Right? I kept asking every single day, and she always acted like she'd forgotten ..."

A disquieting thought suddenly gripped her heart and stole her words as reason and emotion fought to reign her heart.

"You never knew I was out, right?"

She studied their faces in the gathering gloom of the woods. She heard the nearby sound of lapping water striking rock in the nearby fjord.

Would they drown her there? Is that why they'd come this way? How could those she loved be so cruel?

"We needed Sigdis to believe certain things," Tekla finally answered, by way of mercy. "Mostly that we considered you corrupted."

Norill began to breathe again as her thoughts outpaced her emotions.

"Why?" she asked the others in a small, frightened voice she barely recognized as her own.

Her mother at last knelt and embraced her child.

After all she had just been through, the embrace was at once welcome and repugnant. She could sense the older woman's emotional release. Tekla dispassionately surveyed their surroundings looking for any indication they were being watched.

"Oh, Norill, you're still my dear child. Their lies only have power if we believe them. A false face can be just as powerful. Your cell was targeted. You were targeted but left free to draw in others to their own destruction before they deal with you. This was not done by accident. There was an intent. A conspiracy that we believe comes from within the Norwegian resistance. Someone is working their own dark designs to expose us all, or to sow such chaos and distrust that we cripple the resistance ourselves," her mother asserted.

"Gerntz?" Norill hazarded. "If he is a double agent …."

They were all lost in thought for a time.

"How long have you been in the resistance?" Norill finally asked the women.

"Your mother and I are in a cell. Erickson was our third," Tekla said, the sorrow creeping into her voice. "If someone is now targeting us, we figured it was best to establish your loyalties and to bring you in as our third."

"But why would you trust me now?" Norill challenged. "The facts haven't changed. The others from my cell are still dead or missing. Gerntz is still an unknown. I'm still a liability to the cause."

Her mother drew them both up.

"You are my daughter," her mother smiled as she clasped her hands lovingly on either side of Norill's face. "You have many talents, my angel, but acting has never been one of them. And if I'm wrong, I'd rather die fighting for you, with you, then abandon you to become part of the inhuman machinations of the Nazi state."

The two women held each other's gaze, in shared warmth, and love for the other.

"We should go," Tekla noted. "We've only got twenty minutes until curfew."

"Where should I stay?" Norill hurriedly asked as the others began to retrace their steps along the path.

"Both our rooms are likely under surveillance," Tekla remarked to Norill's mother. "I don't know that it matters."

The older woman paused.

"No, it does. I'm angry at my daughter so she should stay with you. I'll leave first. If someone is watching, it will look like you were simply trying to play peacemaker between us tonight. All must appear as it has been. We'll talk in a few days," she added before turning to leave.

"And Rejor?" Norill quietly asked, halting her mother's steps.

She never turned, only lowered her head a fraction as she spoke over her shoulder.

"What I told you before is shamefully true. Perhaps one day when this is all over, we will be able to erect a marker for both him and your father."

**

Norill spent several days running about town attempting to settle her brother's affairs. She closed financial accounts, signed legal documents for his newspaper, paid off his remaining debts, including his gambling losses, and spent a lonely afternoon selecting and packing items from his apartment that held sentimental value. As she worked, she encountered long-forgotten objects and pictures that bore testimony to the narrative of his life.

The sled he'd built with their father, his framed first published article, a picture of the two of them laughing climbing trees as children, the pocket watch he'd purchased to celebrate the opening of his business, his favorite decorative drinking mug, pictures with friends, two pictures with he and Lisbeth – all these bore witness to happier times.

Her right thumb came to rest over her brother's chest in the image as she whispered his name to the silence. Norill knew some of his demons as well. Unconsciously, she slowly shook her head as deep emotions consumed her. They'd been so close when they were younger.

What had happened to them?

They talked regularly, knew basically what was going on in each other's lives, but at some point, he'd largely hidden himself behind the walls we all build in life. They became so impenetrable over time that the past six years had only brought more and more distance between them.

First his gambling issues, the fights he'd get into, his mysterious marriage, then Lisbeth's disappearance, and finally the stresses of the war, all had taken him from being a reserved but fun person to someone she could barely connect with at times. He'd become bitter and self-tortured.

But why was he dead?

Had he been eliminated by the same traitor destroying resistance cells? From a fight or debts he had incurred? Or was his ending tied to whatever had become of Lisbeth?

It seemed, finally, only questions remained.

Norill paused and carefully examined both photos that Lisbeth appeared in. She was shorter than Rejor, with a pleasant face, auburn hair, and a curvy figure.

No, wait. It was more than that.

A disquieting notion filled Norill as she removed the

photos from their frames hoping to find a date on either. She found none but the physical change from one picture to the other was unmistakable. She pondered the images very carefully, her few memories of the woman raced repeatedly through her mind.

"Was she pregnant?" Norill wondered aloud to herself.

Their relationship had always been so secretive, almost as if she were embarrassed of being with Rejor. How long had they been together?

If only she'd been around Lisbeth more, Norill might have a hope of figuring something out, but she and Rejor had kept to themselves, so details were sparse. But Lisbeth had been close to Norill's mother.

For the next hour, Norill turned Rejor's apartment upside down searching for Lisbeth's belongings or any type of clues about their life together. In the end, she could find only three remaining items tucked away in a box in his closet: his wedding band, the torn up remains of a letter written in braille, and an unused train ticket to Oslo, dated ten days before the Nazi invasion of Norway.

***

"And for those who knew him, Gustav Erickson will be greatly missed but he will live forever in our hearts. Amen."

And with those simple words the ceremony concluded.

Norill couldn't help but feeling like there should be more but there wasn't. Just the inevitable ending that all must face in time. How comforting would it be if Rejor was afforded such a final honor so family and friends could properly give voice to their departed? But the Nazis ....

She could not continue.

Her eyes involuntarily tracked towards Mr. Erickson's wife. The woman's face was inscrutable, but Norill couldn't help but feel that she also needed more words of reassurance and solace. Or maybe, Norill just needed to bond with another who was experiencing the loss of a loved one as well.

They'd both, in their own ways, loved this man, and ceremonial words were a poor substitute for what was now lost to each of them. If only there'd been time for her to arrange that kind offer for dinner that he'd extended to her and her mother.

Norill struggled as she pondered the realities of life.

Mr. Erickson had been a good man, one who had always looked out for her. Now she wished she'd told him more often how much his steady support truly meant to her when he'd been alive. How often the habits and pace of daily life silence such generous thoughts as time becomes an endless string, and one cannot envision a day when changes will suddenly come.

Norill wrung her hands as she returned her full attention to the grieving widow as she walked past on the aisle. She would make it a point to talk to her now that formal service was concluded. But at present, she must wait. The church was packed with mourners, but also spies, or sycophants like Sigdis, who'd attempted to sit near her, with her Nazi soldiers, ever vigilant when crowds gathered.

Norill knelt as others, including Tekla and her mother, began to vacate the benches around her. All she sought in her heart was a moment's peace.

Norill had been surprised when it was announced that the service would take place in the same small church, she'd spent time in the day her family farm was stolen. The same church where the mysterious holy man had urged her to visit when he'd passed along the last cryptic indicator that Allied commandos still needed help from the Norwegian resistance. But between dealing with her mother and Tekla, poor Mr. Erickson's horrific fate, her brother's mysterious passing, and Vinni's unknown fate, there had been precious little time to chase phantoms.

"Quite a service," Sigdis' voice wistfully declared from behind her. "Strange to think how we're here one minute and gone the next, but that's life I suppose. How are you holding up?"

Inwardly, Norill sighed.

Despite her best efforts, Sigdis continued to seek her out as often as possible, particularly in public, watching her and keeping doubts about Norill's character and loyalty alive. But there was little Norill could do about it. The Nazi soldier, now permanently on display by Sigdis' side made a confrontation of any sort all but impossible.

Norill took her time to acknowledge the other woman's presence as she slowly stood.

"Oh, Sigdis. Yes, forgive me. I was lost in thought. I'm fine," she moved to exit the row but Sigdis fell into step next to her as they walked up the main aisle toward the door.

"How long had you worked for Mr. Erickson?" Sigdis inquired.

Norill considered her response.

"I worked at the shop during my schooling, but in this capacity, maybe three years or so."

They continued in silence for several steps.

"I see. Well, I suppose you'll have to find a new job, under these unfortunate circumstances. Perhaps, I could be of some assistance with that." Sigdis's offer was accompanied by a pleasant smile.

"Perhaps," Norill agreed noncommittedly, mirroring Sigdis's smile as they reached the doors and exited into muted afternoon sunlight.

"I do hope it won't rain," Sigdis commented as she considered the heavens.

"Excuse me," Norill hastened to the receiving line her mother and Tekla were departing.

For once, Sigdis had the good sense not to follow her as Norill sought out the grieving widow.

The women clasped hands.

"Mrs. Erickson, I'm so sorry about Gustav. He was such a good man and I truly enjoyed working for him very much. I will miss him terribly. The whole town will."

Norill reflected how feeble her words felt under the circumstances. They'd met of course, off and on over the years that she'd worked at the shop, but those encounters seemed a lifetime ago. Still, a kind, sad, appreciative smile greeted Norill's statement.

"Thank you, Norill. I know you and Tekla were special to him too. He loved this church," she added as she turned her gaze back to the humble edifice. "He'd come here often when he was troubled."

They both stood in reflective contemplation of the nearby structure, now all but empty as a steady parade of cars continued to depart. It was then that the first drops of rain began to fall. Without thought, Norill ran to the car her mother and Tekla had piled into.

"Mother give me your umbrella," she hurriedly bid, departing the car as soon as it was in her grasp.

She raced back to Mrs. Erickson as the tentative drops were replaced by more intense ones and began to escort the older woman to her nearby car.

"Have you sought any absolution or spiritual comfort today?" Mrs. Erickson asked in hushed tones as they huddled underneath the umbrella. Norill fervently shook her head.

"Just in my prayers."

The older woman casually lowered the umbrella to quickly obscure their faces from prying eyes.

"Do so. In the church, now," she urgently implored the younger woman as the downpour worsened just as they reached the car. "Watch out for the clergyman. He sees only the good he thinks he can do, and not the true realities of this world. His heart is pure, but he is a pawn, and one who does not know it. This makes him dangerous."

The women paused in voiceless, mutual recognition.

By now, only two vehicles remained, aside from Mrs. Erickson's: the one with Tekla and her mother and the Nazi vehicle containing Sigdis. The rain grew harder. Norill got in the widow's car. They backed up to maneuver as the other cars did as well. Intent on leaving and with the storm's intensity obscuring views, this was the time for her to escape.

"The fence child," Mrs. Erickson bid recognizing the fleeting opportunity.

She imperceptibly slowed as Norill jumped from the open door and crouched low behind the end of the fence that surrounded the churchyard. The rain was freezing, but neither of the other vehicles paused to indicate that anyone had taken notice of her sudden absence from the widow's car. She waited patiently as the rain somehow fell even harder, making sure everyone was long departed before she headed back inside the church.

Norill shivered, as a large puddle of water formed beneath her in the entryway. From here, she could see the dim glow of a candle from one side of the confessional. Noiselessly, she crossed the rows to the other side of the church, lit a candle, and entered the vacant side.

She paused.

Her heart was racing, and her voice trembled a little as she continued to shiver from her cold, damp clothing.

"Please hear my confession and pronounce …," she began.

"If you flee you will be killed," a familiar, unwelcome voice informed her. "You must listen to what I have to tell you. After that, do what you will."

She peered uselessly at the obscuring screen but could

not make out the form she sought on the other side.

"Your being here will get us killed," Norill cried out in confusion, disbelief, and horror.

It took every ounce of emotional strength she possessed not to flee from the church immediately.

"Quiet!" the disembodied voice ordered in a harsh, hushed tone. "Quiet."

"Gerntz, I can't do this," Norill confessed after several tense seconds of stillness.

"You can," he assured her, his tone softening. "You must if you are to save yourself, for you are in grave danger."

She breathlessly waited.

The pause seemed eternal before Gerntz spoke again.

"Tekla, your mother, they are not what they seem. They are leading you into a trap. A glider did crash on your mother's property. There are Allied troops from the crash buried in unmarked graves in the yard of this very church. They will take any action to expose whoever is destroying the resistance, even against you."

Norill fought to reconcile her conflicting feelings.

"How did you escape?" she finally managed.

There was a long pause.

"I tried to save her before I resorted to bribing the guards," Gerntz responded after an infinite silence. "Your friend, Vinni. She has been shipped off to a camp as an undesirable. You will not see her again. I'm sorry."

Norill felt her breath escape but she couldn't draw it back in, so intense was the pain.

"Others are fighting to help," Gerntz added. "Allied commandos do need your help. Do not abandon them."

"How can I possibly help them?" Norill plead, unsure in that moment what she truly felt, but there was no answer. "If my own friends and family don't trust me, what chance do I have?"

The heartbeats in her chest marked the seconds but still she waited.

"Your brother is alive," Gerntz finally responded.

Norill's chest seized with these words.

"What? Where is he, where is he?!" she desperately repeated as her breath escaped in rapid, uncontrollable gasps, but there was no answer.

Moved by a complex host of emotions she'd never felt at once, she ripped back the curtain from her humble booth, but when she withdrew the other side's concealing cloth there was but a flickering candle, all but down to the nub. All she could do was stand there and shiver as no movement in any part of the church presented her with a path to follow.

**

There was but a gentle mist now falling as Norill absently waded into the graveyard. Her mind fixed on a singular task. Her dear sister was buried here. She stalked about the churchyard, adrift in long-repressed memories as she sought her past.

Fierce and unrelenting doubts plagued her mind as she sought the final resting place of her departed family member. Though she looked for her long-lost sister, her thoughts tended upon Rejor.

Was it possible that he lived, as Gerntz maintained?

If so, then why such deception? Or was it, like the assertion that her mother and Tekla intended to betray her, an elaborate trap intended to get her to bring about the downfall of those she loved most?

Gerntz.

Why had he saved her the day she'd gone to the farm for honey? Could he truly be what he claimed, a spy for the Allies? How had he gained Mrs. Erickson's trust to send her to him? Had she even known he'd be there?

"Can I help you, Ms. … oh," the clergyman stopped in surprise recognition as Norill turned to face him. They said nothing to each other as his eyes warily darted about their surroundings. "Afraid when the rain started, I was out in the shed beyond the churchyard and got stuck there for a time. Have you been here long?"

Norill considered if she should mention Gerntz, who'd vanished like a wraith.

Could he be here watching them? Was this clergyman to be trusted? The warning given by Mrs. Erickson echoed in her thoughts.

She summoned a subdued smile.

"I stayed after the service and when the rain started tried to wait it out in the church. My youngest sibling was lain to rest here many years ago. I'm afraid I've forgotten the exact spot; I can only seem to recall a small angel as part of the marker," Norill professed as she slicked back sopping wet strands of hair.

The clergyman considered her a moment.

"I may have a spare coat in the church. If you'd like to go back …"

"No, no," Norill stepped away from his outstretched hand, offered in escort. "I'll be fine. Do you know of the grave I'm searching for? Haugen? The last name is Haugen. Asta Haugen."

The man again paused before walking away, speaking over his shoulder.

"I'm going to go and get an umbrella and consult the records. Then we'll find it together."

*

Norill tried her best not to saturate the hem of her dress in the mud but the damp shifting earth, coupled with her heeled shoes made her efforts all but impossible. Finally, she knelt on one knee to clear debris from the fractured stone outside the churchyard. Her memory was so much stronger of it than the actual object before her was. Now only two letters and the tips of the angel's wings remained etched into the weathered marker.

She pondered the fate of the stone.

Nature had all but erased traces of her sister's existence, just as the Nazis had done to Rejor. One day, this would happen to her.

Who would mourn her, tend to her memory?

"I'm sorry, Kjære Haugen. It seems the records weren't the only source of neglect by my predecessor. Looks like the tree roots are largely to blame," the clergyman surmised as he sympathetically surveyed the gravestone or rather the remnants of one.

They'd discovered her sister's burial place in the far back corner of what had once been the old churchyard. At some point, the fence line had been replaced and moved forward from this spot. The graves here forgotten. A massive tree had grown over the years, its roots now well established, overspread the area, dislodging and, in some cases, damaging the markers of other departed loved ones.

"I'd like to be alone a little while," Norill quietly said.

"I understand. I'll be in the church offices," the other uttered.

She heard the clergyman leave.

*

For a long time, Norill knelt in quiet stillness, her heart and mind aflame.

What should she do next?

Whatever cruel web she'd been caught in seemed to be rapidly closing in around her.

Endgame.

Could she hope to survive, and if so, as what?

To move from this place invited the future, one now so dark and obscured, she wished only to overleap the fated steps to come. Death now walked with her, a living thing, intent only upon its own mysterious, atrocious designs.

Still, she must know the grace of light in this world again. Let it pass, let this all pass Norill prayed as she lowered her head.

"I wish you were here," she softly said to the fractured marker that bore testimony to her sister's short life. Images of an imagined life with her adult sister adorned her thoughts, bringing a fresh sense of loss and isolation. Norill lightly kissed the fingers of her right hand before she placed them lovingly on the stone and rested them there.

"Watch over me," she bid.

Norill rose and began to walk slowly back toward the church. As she did so the rain again, accordingly, increased in intensity. Dismayed, Norill began to weave a creative path back to the church, seeking additional refuge under trees, wishing she'd not rejected the repeated offers of the clergyman to take his umbrella. She was so wet at this point she couldn't fathom why it would matter, but the current deluge forced her to confront a fundamental truth.

Honest though the offers may have been, she didn't trust the clergyman any more than she trusted anyone else right now. Even over something as innocuous as a simple as the offer of a common umbrella danger now lurked. It was a kindness shown her, one she dare not trust. Enemies, danger, and intrigue shifted and changed form seemingly from minute to minute in the grim reality she now faced.

A low rumble of dull thunder echoed across the sky as she

paused yet again beneath a tree, not too far from the churchyard proper. She knelt upon the saturated ground, trembling, waiting for some sign it was safe to proceed.

She hoped Gerntz was trapped somewhere in this deluge. The thought brought a smile of satisfaction to her lips. It was the least he deserved after such a prolonged period of emotional torment.

Her eyes roved carelessly across the nearby landscape.

This was a newer area of the churchyard so there'd been no need to spend time here earlier as they'd searched for her sister's final resting place. There was nothing to note here.

No. No, they fixed upon something her mind could not easily process. Silk? A military boot? What was she seeing protruding from the nearby ground?

Reluctantly, she began to scratch at the loose earth. Answers. She needed answers in this shallow grave.

They revealed themselves faster than anticipated.

A man dressed in an Allied uniform lay concealed beneath the soil. He was not alone.

Norill's tired eyes traveled studiously over the landscape. Her heart sank.

There were others, crudely buried but present nonetheless. The deluge must have washed away dirt from these hastily constructed graves.

The Allied commandos in need of saving?

Her shaking hand sought her forehead as she pondered the dark possibilities. The clergyman was laying a trap. Gerntz was responsible for these deaths. What of her mother and Tekla's roles? Or could another unseen force seek her demise?

Her soul felt poisoned.

What was the right course?

Anger surged as she unconsciously struck her fist into the damp dirt. She was sick of being toyed with. Norill charged through the downpour.

She'd have her answers.

As she passed the far side of the church, her progress was unexpectantly arrested by the appearance of a Nazi staff car parked in front of the building. From her concealed location, she watched and waited.

The clergyman was ardently speaking with the officer beneath the shared umbrella. The exchange was both heated and benign. The Nazi clearly wanted something but was unwilling to bring the full might of the Third Reich upon the weak man he confronted so the understated threats and protests continued as they spoke. Seizing the opportunity, Norill retreated into the church, intent at last on a course of action.

She wanted the clergyman's car keys ... and a coat.

**

It was nearing dusk. Rain pinged dully off the metal roof of the car, cascading in sheets down the windshield. Norill sat inside, staring absently.

Was this the right choice? Had she lost her mind?

Her fingers flexed unconsciously against the stiff steering wheel of the parked vehicle. She'd waited over an hour for the Nazi to leave the church and then even longer to be certain no one else might be watching. The clergyman never reappeared after going back into the house of worship.

Maybe the Nazi had killed him. Perhaps they were in league. Now, none of it mattered for her next actions could easily render such considerations secondary.

Instead of returning to town, Norill had driven here. How long had it been since she'd visited the back sections of what had been her family's vast property?

In her youth, Norill's father had regularly taken she and Rejor hiking here. They'd tracked elk and other animals and spent fun, relaxing hours together – a true family.

The memories faded.

Only danger and likely death now waited for her once she got out of the car and crossed onto the illegitimate domain of the Third Reich.

Still, she must know.

Steeling herself, Norill exited the car, once more surrendering herself to the storm's damp, unwelcoming embrace. Although she had found a portable light in the car, she dare not use it.

Who knew what types of patrols now haunted these woods?

Stealth was her only option and soon the gathering gloom would curtail any chance she had to act, and she highly doubted she'd ever be able to reach this place again. Hunching her shivering shoulders, Norill hesitated briefly before ducking beneath the old gate across the driveway.

At first, she moved with caution.

Every errant sound sent her crouching toward the ground, her eyes rapidly flickering across the landscape, seeking danger, heart pounding. But no one appeared, and soon the reality of time offered her fewer and fewer chances to indulge in much subterfuge. The property was vast. Finding a downed Allied glider in the slowly descending gloom suddenly seemed to be a very foolish and daunting notion.

The trees grew denser as she walked, the forest darkened.

She sensed the danger only seconds before a body slammed her to the ground, landing crushingly on top of her. She struggled but the Nazi soldier was much stronger than her. Norill cried out as his elbow struck her ribs and she drew air in haltingly. Terrified, she pummeled the man as best she could in the neck. He reached for his gun. At first her efforts appeared to do little, but suddenly he lurched back, clasping at his throat and sending the gun tumbling to the ground. Norill dove for it.

Out of nowhere, a shadowy figure emerged, grabbing the Nazi by his neck. Norill rolled and swiped the abandoned gun from the ground. It wavered as the men struggled. Then, a sickening sound testified to the pressure applied to the Nazi soldier's neck as his struggles abruptly ceased and the man standing over him crudely and harshly dropped the body to the ground.

Norill met the man's eyes as she took aim at him.

"Shoot me and you'll bring the rest of them down on us," Gerntz sincerely cautioned as he intensely searched their surroundings, waiting for another assault.

"Don't think I won't," Norill challenged, her hands shaking with both adrenaline and from the cold, persistent rain.

Gerntz met her eye and held it.

"You won't," he judged as he waited to see what she'd do. "You couldn't before."

Norill's heaving breaths bore testimony to the struggle within as she beheld Gerntz over the dead Nazi soldier. That day when the soldiers had intercepted her outside of town was different. This time there was no one present to stop her.

She should kill him now. End this terror here.

"We're close to the Allied glider," Gerntz cautiously announced, his eyes fixed on the gun in the young woman's hands. "I can guide you the rest of the way if you put that down."

"Why would you help me?" she challenged, a grim laugh choking her words. "To lead me into another trap? To give me false evidence? Why do you want to destroy me?!"

Gerntz slowly sat on the other side of the dead soldier.

"I told you. I'm a double agent. Right now, you're my best chance for survival. The Nazis will kill me if they find me. The Allies are my best chance to live. And they're your best chance as well. How long do you think you can survive in Norway now that you've been drawn into the Nazis' plans, eh? If they don't kill you, the resistance will. You're smart, Norill. Smarter than most. That's why you're still alive. We're both caught in something much bigger than ourselves. If we help each other, we might both just live. Please," he implored.

"You're a selfish drittstøvel," Norill scoffed as she finally relaxed her aim. "What did you tell the men on the road that day? Why make me try to shoot that bird?"

Gerntz allowed himself a tight smile.

"I'd forgotten about that. I told them you were the greatest threat in Norway."

Norill turned her head in puzzlement.

"They tracked you through the checkpoints. My superior got a call that you were heading out of town and sent me to find you."

"The one who took my family's land?" Norill confirmed.

"The same. He wants to crush Allied and resistance strength in this area and thinks your mother is central to it. I bluffed them. If you'd shot and proven you knew how to use a gun, they'd have dealt with you then. I took a chance that you weren't that stupid, and it paid off long enough for me to show them my commander's order that you only be detained by me."

Neither spoke as the rain pelted them.

"You're an even bigger drittstøvel," Norill asserted as she motioned at Gerntz.

"One you need alive," he reminded her.

Awkwardly, they stood as she resumed keeping the gun trained on him.

"Where's the glider?" she demanded.

A disquieting smile greeted her question.

"Which one?" Gerntz smugly asked.

*

They traveled in virtual silence as they temporarily broke out of the woods and began to clamber up a rocky hillside. Norill struggled to keep her footing on the damp stones. When she'd dressed this morning, it had been for a very different purpose. But ruined clothing seemed a small price to pay for desperately needed answers.

Gerntz was moving faster and his shadowy form kept pausing, waiting for her to catch-up. Hopefully, he couldn't tell that she'd had to pocket the gun.

"How much further?" she anxiously asked as they crouched down on a ledge. Her lower legs burned, she was exhausted and beyond sick of the ceaseless, miserable rain.

"Actually, we're here," he declared evenly. "Look up, to the left," he instructed without having to read her puzzled expression.

Shielding her eyes against the drops, Norill gazed where directed but to no avail. Abruptly, he was pulling her closer. The movement was so unexpected she offered little resistance; instead, her eyes followed his arm to the tip of his finger to a point far up in the trees.

Sure enough, several unmistakable shapes hovered there.

"How long has it been there," she wondered aloud.

"Hard to say," Gerntz admitted, catching his breath. "I'd guess several weeks to well over a month. The other glider's in the woods. They keep guards and sharpshooters stationed near it hoping that one of the surviving Allied soldiers or a useful resistance member comes. I don't know if they've spotted this one. It's pretty well-hidden, even in the daylight."

"How did you find it?" Norill questioned.

He offered nothing in return.

"We should leave," he contended, moving away from her as he said so.

Norill ignored his sentiments and pressed onward. Perhaps there was something more she could discern from the ground.

Arriving at the top of the hillside, she was immediately hit by strong gales of both wind and rain. She slipped to the ground as they buffeted her but still, she kept going. The trees offered a bit of respite, still she knew that she must search quickly.

What could she hope to find?

The ground was soft and full of roots and rock, so footprints would be all but impossible. A disturbing, ominous groan from above shot her heart into her throat. She breathlessly looked up and traced the form of the shadowy wreck high above; it obviously wasn't secure there.

If the right gust of wind shifted the trees or the glider, it would come down.

Heedless of the danger, she cast about in the rain-choked torrent of darkness. She'd come too far, lost too much to leave this place with nothing to show for her efforts.

The dead, the missing demanded it.

"We have to leave," Gerntz urgently repeated from behind her. "It's not safe and you're going to freeze to death out here."

It was then that something caught her eye and Norill lurched toward it, only halting in her tracks when she was a few steps away. Her eyes fought to put into context what might be before her as Gerntz closed the distance between them.

It was the flapping of the parachute that had attracted her attention.

"It's just a dead man," Gerntz shouted over her shoulder.

"We need to get his tags ...,"

Norill never finished the thought, dimly aware of an object striking her head as she fell, completely senseless long before hitting the unforgiving ground.

**

"Slowly, slowly, "the gentle male voice admonished.

Norill could feel the cold-water coursing down her constricted throat. The tone of voice was at once comforting, familiar, and out of place. Her mind's eye played out the final seconds locked into her memory.

Frigid wind. An obscuring night. Gerntz. The sound of creaking metal above. Blackness.

Her eyes shot painfully open, desperate for answers in response to the images and sounds that had just assaulted her memory.

Within a matter of seconds her dull, shifting mind tentatively confirmed that she was clearly once again within the confines of the church she'd left hours earlier.

Hours? Was she sure?

Norill blinked repeatedly as she fought to regain focus on her vision.

"How long have I been out?" her hoarse voice uttered.

"Long enough. For a moment, I feared we'd lost you," the holy man confessed.

"What happened to me?" Norill groggily asked.

There was only the slightest of hesitations before the other replied.

"Gerntz said you were struck by a falling piece of debris from the glider."

Norill fought to taste the sensation of moisture in her mouth again. Instead, she was greeted to the unmistakable taste of blood in her mouth, which caused her pause before she decided the blow must have caused her to bite her tongue. Her eyes continued their struggle to focus but finally fixed fully upon her attendant.

"Do you believe that's what happened?" she pointedly inquired as pain suddenly shot down her spine.

"I wouldn't try to move," the other advised as she sought a more comfortable position. "Look, I don't know what happened or didn't, only that your companion said you needed to remain here for your own safety."

"The Nazis already came here. How safe can I be?"

Norill wanted urgently to leave, but the shooting pains down her back prevented it.

"What do you know of Gerntz?" Norill continued. "He's a spy, you know. Are you? Why was that Nazi here?" she openly challenged.

"You're feverish," the man replied, with both a haunted and dismissive look.

"Why won't you answer my questions?"

The man stood as a host of conflicting thoughts and emotions played across his face.

"Stay here," he bade at last before exiting the modest room. Norill was mildly surprised she didn't hear the turning of a key in the lock to contain her.

She tried to focus beyond the physical pain.

What was happening here?

Could Gerntz possibly be telling the truth?

The hastily buried bodies of Allied soldiers in the graveyard, the confirmed presence of a second glider, the glaring fact that she hadn't already been turned over to the Nazis, the coded message in the Ibsen book that the Allied soldiers still needed her help, all of it seemed to support that there was a measure of truth to Gerntz's assertations.

Could it be conceivable that somehow her mother and Tekla were actually the ones ready to betray her?

Norill's hand trembled as she raised it toward her throbbing temple.

The image of her poor brother, alive and well, flitted

across her mind as her fingers absently played their tips across her forehead. They would discover no answers there.

Erickson's wife ....

She was the one who'd suggested she go back inside the church after the funeral service. In her mind, Norill ardently fixed upon the image of the older woman's face. A visage at once familiar, simple, trusted, and kind.

Why dear God had she sent her to Gerntz? Indeed, why was her poor husband even dead? Had Mr. Erickson discovered that she was working for the other side and she'd played a hand in his gruesome demise?

The thought repelled Norill.

No, she trusted that face.

What if she didn't know that Norill would be confronted by Gerntz in the church? The Nazis and their traitorous minions had been manipulating her for months. Could they have done the same to Mrs. Erickson? Made her an unwitting pawn in whatever twisted game they were now mutually ensnared in?

Her thoughts embraced the potential scope of the deceit.

What if all of this was part of a grand deception designed to turn one hidden ally against the other to ensure their shared destruction? If it was so, then the forces working to bring about their downfall must either be clairvoyant or insidiously connected to the Norwegian resistance. A force driven by a twisted mind bent on moving all the pieces precisely into place, utterly savoring the climatic disillusion before them as they did so. Someone who had a point they desperately wanted to make before casting all their unsuspecting victims into fatal confusion before each succumbed to a final deadly darkness.

The cold, calculating cruelty of it all left her mind numb and her soul in turmoil.

Norill steeled herself. She must be the truth – the light

that exposed this craven force before anyone else was drawn into this destructive web of deception.

Her gun was gone. She needed a weapon.

Her eyes vacillated around the modest room. Nothing presented itself until Norill suddenly realized the sheet she clutched would work. Frantically, she tore a length and wound it into a makeshift garrote.

Her erstwhile holy man would tell her the truth, or she'd force it out of him. She paused only an instant as she rose out of bed and beheld a cross mounted on the wall.

How far was she willing to take this?

The door was unexpectedly thrown open, and for a fraction of a second, the looming sight of a wild-eyed man filled her vision before he harshly forced a bag over her head, tumbling her once again into blackness.

**

Her body shuddered.

Blind – she was more than aware she was bound and trapped in the perpetually shifting trunk of a car. The condensation of her breath dampened the rough bag still on her head. The ropes clasped about her wrists and above her ankles were biting, harsh reminders of her vulnerability.

What would happen when the car stopped? Why hadn't she already been executed?

The car turned violently, suspending her thoughts as her right shoulder bore the brunt of the ensuing impact against some object. Norill gasped as the harsh impact coursed down the nerves of her arm and up her neck. It was then repeated three more times. She promised herself she wouldn't cry, even as unbidden tears raced down her cheeks.

Her surroundings began to pitch even more sharply. They must have left whatever paved road they'd been traveling.

The jarring motions of the fast-moving vehicle tossed her stomach into fits. Her very bones reverberated with each jolting bounce.

Then the vehicle abruptly slammed to an unceremonious stop.

Norill's chest heaved in anticipation and fear as within the span of a few seconds, the muted sounds outside suddenly broke through at full volume as the trunk opened. A hand smashed down awkwardly on her face.

Was she screaming?

More unwelcome hands fumbled across her body before gaining purchase and began lifting Norill toward her fate.

She would die. Norill knew she would die.

Her breath now escaped in gasps and fits as tears raced across her face and unspoken regrets surged through her fragile mind.

How could it already be her end?

She was being manipulated again. Even sightless, she could tell she'd been moved inside as her staggered steps echoed dully off unseen walls. Her head swung wildly as the sounds of her own muted protest greeted her ears.

She must escape.

Norill's shoes scraped vigorously against the wooden floor in frantic protest as she was awkwardly dragged before being forced downward onto a seat.

"No! Please God, please God …," she desperately repeated as the bag was unceremoniously ripped from her head.

She was helpless.

"I'm sorry, I'm sorry," Norill cried as her eyes blinked uselessly against the unexpected mixture of shadowy figures and light that assaulted her senses.

The closest figure grabbed her face and cradled it. Terrified beyond rational thought, the man had to say her name several times before realization began to dawn.

"Gerntz?"

She reflexively heaved backward in alarm.

"Yes, yes, Norill. Calm down. You're safe now," the familiar voice promised.

"You're lying!" she spat as she struggled against his tentative grasp.

How could this man possibly be telling the truth?

Turning outward, she failed to break free and ended up sagging her body forward at an awkward, downward angle to his. She was so tired. Every nerve in her body desperately beckoned her for rest.

The hours in the rain, cold and wind, the injury to her head, the rough and unpleasant trip to wherever she now found herself, coupled with ceaseless psychological pressures threatened to finally overwhelm her frail state as Gerntz lifted her fully upright and turned her to him once again.

He held up military tags.

"They're from the glider wreck. I've brought you to your friends. Your Allied friends," he asserted fervently before continuing. "They are scheduled to leave Norway and have vowed to take you with them. You're free, Norill. Free. The war is over for you."

Gradually, she turned her head and beheld the handful of men that surrounded them before returning her gaze fully upon Gerntz in astonished disbelief.

"Free? It's over?" she quietly questioned as her breathing unconsciously slowed.

"Yes. They're taking you to England," Gerntz smiled reassuringly as he released her.

Had she ever seen this man truly smile?

"How can they be taking me to England when they can't even escape this country themselves? I've seen the bodies ...."

"It's true," a British accented voice interrupted from behind Norill. She turned and assessed the stubble-covered face of the speaker. The striking blue eyes were unforgettable.

"The café," she quietly said as recognition dawned.

"Yes, I gave you both messages," the other confirmed. "When your cell was compromised, I feared the worst, but Gerntz was able to secure us food, shelter, clothing, and eventually radio equipment so we could send for help."

Norill turned upon Gerntz.

"How could you know? I never told anyone about those messages," she darkly insisted.

Gerntz drew in a breath.

"Haven't you wondered whatever happened to the third member of your cell, Haktor?"

Norill momentarily looked away before solemnly nodding.

"He knew you all were in danger but didn't know how to get out. As it turned out, I'd previously worked with and befriended a few of his contacts in the resistance during my time in Norway. He'd already reached out to them in order to secure safe passage for you out of the country. I have better Allied contacts and used them to reach out to Haktor. He's now safe in England. I began spying on you when I learned you planned to leave. I witnessed your hasty encounter in the café and pursued this man back to his comrades."

"At great peril," one of the men added to the shared, unspoken agreement of the others.

Though they now wore civilian clothing, this short statement confirmed in Norill's mind that she was in the company of professional soldiers. Something in their body language conveyed both conviction, comradery, and an underlying deadly earnestness, which left no room for question.

"Again, I was able to use my position both with the Allies and Nazis to advantage. Knowing where they were, I was able to divert German patrols from this area, falsify reports, and use my Allied contacts to begin planning their rescue," Gerntz explained. "Haktor was invaluable in supplying the radio equipment."

Norill's eyes drifted to where Gerntz indicated. A partially concealed wireless radio set was just visible behind a standing screen. She afforded herself the opportunity to examine the rest of her surroundings.

She was in a medium sized room of a cabin. A crackling fire burned low in the fireplace, emitting little in the way of either smoke, light, or warmth. The room was sparse and cramped. The few windows in sight were covered with heavy curtains.

"We sent the second message, so you'd know we hadn't perished and that you'd keep investigating," said the soldier Norill had first met at the café.

"So, I was a decoy? A way to keep the Nazis busy?"

There was a collective pause.

"Haktor wanted you out. He informed us of the recent unexplained elimination of resistance cells," the apparent Allied leader stated.

"We had to know where your loyalties actually laid before we attempted to take you with us," another added.

She reflected on this before nodding in understanding.

"And Vinni?" Norill asked hesitantly.

For a march of seconds no one spoke, only the shifting shadows cast by the smoldering fire played across their stoic faces.

"We believe there was a conspiracy to destroy your resistance cell," the lead British commando stated. "We've taken measures to minimize the damage," was the only further explanation offered.

"Is she dead?"

No answer was offered.

"Please, I can't leave without knowing her fate. She's

my friend," Norill begged, but the others turned and resumed whatever tasks they'd been engaged in before her arrival.

She lowered her head in sorrow, even as she gripped it in pain from her previous injury.

"Rest," Gerntz advised as he handed her a thick blanket. "Tonight will undoubtedly be long."

**

Norill jolted awake.

The fog of sleep was slow to clear as her sluggish mind attempted to assign patterns to her dim surroundings. She tried to recall what was happening to her.

For a terrifying instant she feared she was back in Nazi detention. No. She was in a cabin, awaiting evacuation to England. Her head still ached but the pain seemed more manageable.

She breathed deeply, aware of the glistening film of sweat that clung to parts of her skin and clothing. The room was quiet. She was hungry.

What time was it?

The closed blackout curtains offered her no clues. She sighed, heavily.

It was frustrating to be so ancillary to the events that were shortly destined to unfold, especially as they would inexorably and irrevocably alter the fundamental nature of her life. Still, her eyes closed in a tacit prayer of gratitude. At least her body no longer felt as if it was on the verge of collapse.

"It's just as well that you're awake now, Ms. Haugen," a familiar voice near the fireplace declared. "Our hour of liberation is near."

Norill reopened her eyes and considered the previously unseen shadow near the still smoldering fireplace.

"Where are the others?" she managed, realizing how thirsty she was as she spoke.

Her mysterious companion must have heard the parched nature of her words for he wordlessly stood and crossed the room to retrieve her a cup of water.

"The others have already left. We must follow soon," he noted as he finished pouring water from the pitcher before carrying the cup over to her. "Would you like to eat something?"

She drank deeply, reflecting on all she'd done and witnessed since the last drops of water had graced her lips. The cup was refilled several times. Life returned to her body with each cool sip.

"Why didn't you answer my question about Vinni?" Norill demanded the final time she handed the cup back to the soldier.

The man lightly hefted the cup in his large hand, as if measuring it as he wrestled with some hidden internal impulse.

"You may yet see her again," was all he was initially able to bring himself to reveal.

For a matter of heartbeats, Norill feared that was to be all, but he reluctantly continued.

"At Gerntz's insistence, we tasked a handful of our party to rescue her by derailing the train she was being taken away in several weeks ago. If any of the party survived, they are to meet us tonight at the extraction point with your friend."

"Thank God," Norill whispered, as her heart bathed in quiet gratitude. "Thank God."

Suddenly afraid this conversation was some veiled trap she returned her attention fully to her companion.

"Do you trust Gerntz?"

The other was quiet as only the crackle from the small fire intruded the moment.

She waited.

"He has been a great help, and we have few friends with

real resources in this country," he asserted.

"But do you trust him?" she persisted.

The soldier seemed to have similar misgivings as her own for he again paused and threw a cautious glance about the empty room, as if he too feared his next thoughts that were spoken out loud.

"I find it convenient that the same night he escaped the Nazis was the same night we struck the train. Quite the convenient distraction. Brought down what seemed like half the Nazi occupying force to the wreck. It could have been our undoing, and no disrespect to you and your friend, but it was all for an expendable asset from what I can tell," he finished with his back turned to her so Norill could not see the man's emotion, only sense it in his voice.

"You said this attack on the train was several weeks ago?" she bid.

He nodded.

The image of the surreal dinner at Sigdis' household returned fully to her mind. The harried exit of so many high-ranking Nazi officers hadn't made any sense at the time.

Could they have been responding to the mutual misfortunes of Gerntz's escape, coupled with the disastrous news of a prison train being ambushed in a country that was supposedly under the oppressive boot of the Third Reich?

While the notion brought her grim pleasure, other darker thoughts roamed her mind like torrents of black, thick smoke coursing wildly down an enclosed hallway.

"How did Gerntz get enough intel to pick that night for the attack? He was with me when we were arrested," Norill wondered aloud.

The two exchanged a staid look but neither gave voice to their suspicions or fears.

"My men are trained to be wary of ambush," the soldier affirmed.

"They will be fine," he added, but Norill couldn't help but think that this final sentiment was spoken as much for his benefit as it was for hers.

"Best get ready, Miss. We leave in one hour."

*

Nazi patrols made the roads far too dangerous, even at night, so they moved as hushed shadows, casting about the remote countryside. The miserable rain had returned making progress slow, their footprints leaving unwelcome visible signs of their clandestine passage.

Her guide stopped so abruptly that Norill almost collided directly into him, but he didn't seem to notice as his head swiveled quickly to ponder their surroundings.

"I need to take a reading," he quietly announced.

They were the first words either of them had uttered since leaving the cabin, in what felt like, hours ago. Norill hunched her shoulders as she crouched down next to the man, who retrieved several items before disappearing under his poncho to conceal his map reading light.

The respite allowed a bevy of thoughts and fears to take hold.

Would she ever see her mother or Tekla again? Did she want to?

In her heart, she still couldn't believe that they could possibly have betrayed her or their country. And yet, right now, she was placing her trust and very life in Gerntz's hands; a man whose mixed loyalties, actions, and credibility were stretched beyond imagination.

How did anyone become so twisted?

Was it by recognizing and accepting that some evils were simply necessary or was it the reality that war strips everyone of morals in different ways?

Her role in the resistance had undoubtedly caused deaths, even if she never heard of them. Before the war such a harsh truth would have undoubtedly horrified her; now it was a fundamental certainty, a part of who she was. In many ways, the person she was before the war was gone, that life a distant memory.

Who had Gerntz been before the war?

Maybe it didn't matter, she thought, as she stared blankly at the concealed form of the Allied paratrooper. Their fates, whatever they were destined to be, were now one.

The man rapidly tossed his cover back, spraying the accumulated water everywhere. Norill remained speechless as his eyes again intensely examined the dark landscape. A fraction of a second after he pointed to indicate the route they must travel, the sound and echo of distant but intense gunfire erupted from the same direction.

They raptly listened, hoping the sounds would provide clarity as to what action they should take. A final, furious cacophony assaulted the night before the former rain-soaked tranquility eerily reasserted itself.

"Where the hell are we going?" Norill demanded as the sudden silence threatened to break their nerves.

The paratrooper held her gaze as they shared a wordless conversation before standing in agreement. They must investigate.

"We'll circle in from the left. Stay low and do everything I tell you to," he ordered as he handed her a pistol. She checked the safety and how many rounds it held, in part to demonstrate that she knew how to use it. The soldier nodded approvingly but paused to appraise her a moment before proceeding.

Did the mortal fear within her betray itself on her face? Was she trembling?

"Be ready for anything," he reluctantly advised as they

renewed their mission.

*

The Nazis obviously had no fear of reprisals for they took no pains to hide their atrocities in the aftermath of carrying out their ambush. From their vantage point above the scene, Norill and her surviving Allied companion huddled in fear and misery, bearing witness to the unholy undertakings below.

Bodies were being crudely piled and counted.

"What's that one doing?" Norill whispered into the Allied soldier's ear. She didn't fail to notice how white the knuckles were that gripped his weapon. Afraid he might be considering something rash, Norill delicately touched his shoulder – she hoped reassuringly.

He may have relaxed only a fraction, but it was enough for him to be able to offer his grim assessment of what was taking place.

"Ambush. Looks like they knew exactly who to expect. The one with the book is probably confirming identities from pictures or something supplied by your Norwegian resistance traitor," he lowered his head a degree, sending rainwater cascading onto the rock they knelt behind.

An icy shiver rose up Norill's spine as she attempted her own count.

The constantly shifting lights held by the enemy soldiers and the dead Nazi bodies mixed in with the others complicated matters. Only a portion of the repulsive scene was backlit by the headlamps of several nearby vehicles. Her efforts were instantaneously halted by the unanticipated appearance of two struggling, masked figures being roughly hauled before the Nazi who appeared to be overseeing this singular massacre.

They watched with bated breath as the concealing bag

was removed from the male member of the pair.

"Captain," Norill's companion's anguish rang out as he said the word.

His body unconsciously lurched forward as he mechanically brought his weapon to bear.

His shot would kill them both.

"No! You'll get us killed," Norill desperately pled in harsh, whispered tones, aware that her words might not even be able to penetrate the man's distressed thoughts.

But she must try. If he pulled the trigger, all was lost.

"Think of the sacrifice of the others. They wouldn't want you to act. Please. You're a soldier. Your duty … think of your duty."

The unmistakable peel of a single shot rent the night. Norill closed her eyes.

She could feel the tears stinging them.

The fool.

But there were no shouts of alarm, only a distant, sickening, dull thud. Dimly, she perceived the soldier in front of her was heaving breaths.

She opened her eyes.

The Allied captain lay prone on the ground – dead. The Nazi commander's Luger pistol smoked visibly against the combined mist and headlights.

"Please," Norill repeated to the lone surviving Allied soldier before her. "Please."

The man held his pose for an eternity before sinking marginally against the boulder beside them. There was nothing he could do except get them killed.

This battle was lost.

Norill again reached out to him, but he recoiled. The deaths of his friends and his own self-reproach were too much for him to allow even the simplest form of comfort.

He was alive, they were dead.

“I’m sorry …,” she began to offer.

“We should go,” he asserted, cutting her off.

“Where? Back to the cabin? To wherever the rendezvous was supposed to take place?” she questioned.

He turned back to face her and for an intense moment they mutually fought the uncertainty within. A return to the cabin was fraught with peril and even if they reached it, what then? However, if they pushed onward, as if nothing had happened, did they willingly walk into an enemy trap as the poor souls below had?

Norill looked away, unable to fathom a clear answer to their shared situation. Any options presented equally negative outcomes in her mind.

Stay here, die.

Return to the cabin, die.

Proceed onward to their original extraction, die?

Her eyes drifted back down to the events playing out below.

The second prisoner!

Norill had nearly forgotten about her plight. The woman was being interrogated by the same Nazi officer who’d shot the Allied Captain. Norill studied the scene with a growing sense of both unease, disbelief, and finally certainty.

“Oh God, Vinni,” she breathed in horror.

“Possibly, “the soldier grimly cautioned. “The others were supposed to convey her from where we’ve been hiding her, but that could be anyone under that hood – a trick to draw us in.”

“You don’t think I recognize her? That’s Vinni,” Norill passionately asserted.

Both suddenly froze thinking the other had heard something behind them over the sound of the rain as they each probed the wooded hillside around them.

“Probably an animal,” Norill uneasily concluded after a

protracted silence.

"We can't stay here," the Allied soldier declared.

Every instinct in Norill told her he was right, but the thought of losing Vinni again was too terrible to comprehend. Her friend's life was at stake.

But hadn't she just prevented such rash action from her companion a few minutes ago when his captain was slaughtered? Could she now be so selfish?

Maybe there was a way ....

"Keep your eyes straight ahead, I'll cover the flanks and rear. Move," the man intensely ordered.

As they began to leave, Norill's heart begged her to take one last gaze at the Nazis below – at her friend. But she knew there could be only one outcome if she did.

They left that hopeless place together as soundlessly as shadows.

*

For a long time, they traveled in combined solitude, each lost in thoughts, sorrows, and relentless questions. The night was endless.

She blinked.

"Are you all right?" the voice was asking her.

At first, Norill didn't even know why the question was being posed until she realized she was sitting in the mud, her leg scraped and bleeding, and one of her shoes was now missing its heel.

A jumble of images and sensations flooded her exhausted mind.

Her heel had caught then broken when it slid down a rock she'd been crossing, pitching her uncontrollably to the ground where she'd, yet again, struck her head. The soldier glanced one final time behind them before bending down to examine first her head then her leg.

"What now?" she finally asked when he was done, holding her hand to the scrape on her temple as he turned his attention to the state of her leg.

"It's not broken," he deflected as he ripped fabric from his clothing in a crude attempt to bandage the wound. "Can't risk leaving a blood trail."

Tying wet cloth proved problematic.

"Dammit, this mission's been cursed since the beginning," he erupted as he threw away the piece of cloth and began to rip another measure from what he was wearing.

Norill didn't speak as he resumed his efforts, obviously embarrassed at his outburst. They could not continue on like this indefinitely. One of them must make the decision.

"What was your mission?" she finally asked as he slumped back after completing his work.

A fleeting wry look flashed across his face before his expression grew more serious.

"I can't see a way out of this, can you?"

She nodded in resigned agreement. He looked away from her.

"The Nazis are building something up here. Some revolutionary weapon that they're pouring a lot of resources into. One that could change everything," he darkly said. "We were supposed to investigate one of their project sites but got intercepted by fighters that drove us off course to crash here. They were on us instantly. No chance we could slip away – at least not en masse."

For an uncomfortable length of time, he gazed intently at her.

"Maybe my mission isn't over. I may not be able to get out, but you still might. Someone needs to take the intelligence we were able to gather back," he nodded. "It may prove to be the key to exposing your traitor in the resistance."

Norill paused.

"How do you know you can trust me?"

"I don't but I don't see another option either," he conceded with a faint smile. "I guess we're down to faith. Do you think you can walk?"

Norill struggled to get up and quickly realized how unsteady she was with the missing heel of her shoe. The soldier grabbed her other shoe, whacked it several times against the nearby stones, and managed to shatter the other heel.

"Come on," he bid, checking his watch. "We can still make it to the extraction point if we hurry."

Before long, Norill was compelled to run barefoot through the freezing rain and mud to keep up.

*

Norill's frame shook uncontrollably as they again hunkered down to survey a scene before them. Without prompting, the soldier held her from behind to try to offer some sense of warmth and comfort. Involuntarily, she sank against him, exhausted.

Her feet burned with both cold and countless abrasions and cuts, but they'd made it to their goal. The ferry was so close.

Freedom was so close.

"When … when does it leave?" Norill managed.

The soldier adjusted his body to be able to gaze upon his watch.

"We'll wait ten minutes," he declared.

The warmth between them was a subtly blissful sensation against the dark, harsh night. These precious moments of stolen peace were to be quietly treasured for Norill knew in the depths of her soul that nothing in her life would ever be the same.

What was ordained would be.

"Do you have a name?" Norill softly asked her benefactor after several minutes of wordless contemplation.

"Corporal Bilson, Miss," he uttered, the response of a conditioned soldier.

"Your name, Corporal," she persisted.

"Edmond. I know … a terrible name. My friends call me Jacks."

"Nice to meet you … Jacks," Norill shuddered in his arms.

Both smiled, content in the shared bond of true connection.

"What will you do if you see the sun tomorrow?" Norill whispered.

The man was lost in emotion.

"Try to remember who I was before I put this uniform on. Eat a steak for breakfast, I suppose. I'd kill for a proper shot of gin right now."

Norill laughed in spite of herself as hope flooded her being that they would see another dawn.

"Breakfast sounds good," she chuckled. "Especially the gin."

"You?" Jacks asked.

Conflicting emotions raced through her as their embrace shifted. Her mind drifted to a future she could only dream of given the grim realities they faced.

"Try like hell to be a better person. Find a cute new pair of shoes. Eat an entire box of cookies. Live," she gently murmured. "Live."

Jacks held her closer against the endless onslaught of rain.

"Tomorrow is yours," he promised. "A ship will intercept you out in the fjord and take you to England."

She was so relaxed that she felt the tension in his muscles

before she fully realized what he was reacting to.

"Oh God," she breathed as her heart began to race at the scene unfolding before them.

They watched in shocked fascination as several German trucks pulled up to the docks and unloaded cloaked figures onto the ferry. The Nazi soldiers appeared to return from the ship, the prisoners did not.

Norill turned to Jacks, only one unspoken question burning between them.

"You have to go," he quietly advised. "There's no future for you here."

Memories of her torture returned to her mind's eye as she gazed into his.

"They want me dead," she asserted.

"They don't even know you're here," he comforted. "Take these. We'll figure out a way to conceal them on you."

He handed her a small bundle of papers.

"They're going to ask questions about my appearance, and I have no travel papers," she recoiled. They'd been all but ruined during her recent travels through seemingly endless deluges.

She was thoroughly drenched, her leg was gashed and bound, a swollen knot protruded from her head, her shoe heels were broken, she was splattered with mud, and freezing cold. She would easily standout from the regular passengers.

Jacks screwed up his lower lip in concentration.

"We were supposed to be supplied with fresh clothes at the original rendezvous point and then filter onto the ferry over time to avoid suspicion. I'm not … wait," he abruptly stood and began to stalk away.

Norill started to struggle to rise but he turned and waved her off before vanishing into the night. Her entire frame trembled. She'd never be warm again.

The young woman hunched her shoulders and began to

rock back and forth to try to keep awake and to generate any type of heat. But her efforts were futile. At this point, her very bones felt saturated. Absent Jacks' body heat there seemed to be little she could do to keep her core warm.

Her mind drifted.

Who were those cloaked figures? Why load them onto this particular ferry on this of all Godforsaken nights? Would the ship be crawling with Nazis or would they leave only a select few behind to guard prisoners? Could she overcome her fear of water and actually will herself onto the ship?

"Wake up, wake up," an urgent, stern voice commanded.

"Wha …," she groggily uttered. "Did I fall asleep? How long was I asleep?"

"Long enough, it took me five minutes to wake you," Jacks admonished. "I brought you a present."

"Where did you get that?" she stammered in surprise.

"Figured the farm we passed would have something like this. Took a bit to scuff it up properly to look the part. Think of it as a pity prop."

"What?" Norill was lost.

Jacks pointed to her injured leg.

"You were trying to bike here in a hurry, and you fell, scraped up your leg, bumped your head, and got drenched. Accident even broke the heels of your shoes," he slyly grinned as he let the deliberately damaged bicycle he'd stolen settle down next to them.

Hope returned to her.

"And what's your cover story?" she wondered aloud, brushing drops away from her eyes.

Jacks grew more somber.

"I'll try to sneak aboard without being noticed, but I'm afraid between my lack of language skills and clothes, I can only hurt your chances. So, this is goodbye."

For an eternity, Norill looked into his eyes before lowering her head. She could not help but feel he was sacrificing himself so that she might survive this terrible night.

"Thank you," she quietly said, too humbled to say more.

The two shared a last, heartfelt embrace, each knowing that the next hour could result in either of their deaths.

"Don't worry. I'll give those Nazi bastards a good fight. Best to get going now, Miss," Jacks advised. "That ferry's not going to wait forever."

He again handed her the bundle of subtly encoded papers, which she promptly did her best to hide on her person.

"I'll see you onboard," Norill's hopeful wish was accompanied by an awkward grin between them.

Then she was gone.

*

"You seem to have had quite the night," a second man smirked at her as she patiently awaited near the rear of the ferry to see if they'd allow her to take a seat onboard.

Norill unconsciously pushed sopping wet hair back behind her ear and lowered her gaze. She was terrified that any second a horde of Nazis would descend upon her, but if she projected that nervousness it would only raise suspicion more quickly.

She both felt and looked wretched, best to play these qualities as the true reason for her discomfort. Let others gawk and speculate, as long as she was allowed safe passage on the ferry; that was all that truly mattered.

The man before her tapped the wet mass of identification papers she'd retrieved from her pocket, now useless due to the rain, as he considered what to do with the distressed woman before him.

"Wait here," he advised before disappearing into a small room behind her.

Norill tried not to focus on the sound of his voice as he put in a call to superiors. Her mind involuntarily flashed back to her time in detention, to the suffering she'd endured, and would do so again if this failed. Or she'd suffer much worse.

Her pulse quickened.

The ship's onboard handset clicked in the cradle a few seconds before the man reappeared.

"Welcome aboard, Miss," he cordially pronounced as he extended a genteel gesture aimed at the nearest seats.

Norill nodded a gracious thanks, carefully considered her surroundings, before selecting a secluded seat apart from the other handful of passengers. Despite the heat in the cabins now showering her with currents of warmth, she shivered almost uncontrollably.

In an attempt to combat this, she shifted her thoughts.

Would Jacks be able to make it onboard?

Her tired eyes roved over the faces arrayed on benches spread across the spacious cabin. Faces.

What had become of the poor, hooded figures who'd been loaded onto this vessel before her? Norill's mind fell into a jumble: the prisoners being forced aboard, the memory of Vinni's face, the stack of bodies in the woods … the countless legions now without a voice.

She wiped tears away, suddenly thirsty.

They deserved better. Humanity deserved better. Somehow, she must survive to fight for a world that would never again know such cruelty again. In this at least there was purpose.

Her desperately frayed nerves suddenly cried out for respite.

Her silent tears turned to those of joy as a new thought flooded her being.

She was free.

Her fatigued eyes turned to consider the dark waters beyond the window. A distant flash briefly illuminated the shifting waters. Tonight, she wasn't even scared of drowning as she concentrated on the deep, rhythmic sound of the idling engines and the warmth of the cabin enveloping her body.

In time, she began to drift off into sleep.

*

CHAPTER FIVE

AN END TO SECRETS

Danger!

Her subconscious mind struggled to process the multitude of sensory inputs assaulting her burgeoning consciousness.

"Disembark, all of you must disembark!" one voice urgently commanded.

"Back to shore. We have engine problems. Back to shore," another higher pitched voice ordered as her eyes flashed opened.

She blinked in disbelief.

This was not a dream, Norill realized, as those on the ferry filed hurriedly and obediently past her. She must wake up.

"Are we sinking," her half-conscious mind articulated as a figure rushed by before pausing.

"No, Miss. But you must return to shore," a uniformed ferryman nearby pressingly advised before he disappeared from view.

Norill stooped to gather the broken shoes she'd deposited on the deck beneath her seat, only to unexpectantly be assaulted from behind as a rough, obscuring bag was thrust upon her head. Unwelcome hands then arms seized her firmly and hauled her upward.

Flailing uncontrollably, Norill staggered backwards. Her bare heels painfully bounced and clanged uselessly against the metal deck.

All Norill could do was to cry out "No!" repeatedly – frantically.

She felt herself propelled backward seconds before her back crashed bluntly into a bench. Her attempt to stand was immediately rebuffed, forcing her downward to her previous position, as her hands were bound in her lap. Norill's mind struggled in vain to seek another means of escape before accepting that there was none.

All that remained was fear.

Everything around her grew deathly quiet; and yet, she knew a concentrated gaze was bearing down on her – waiting, contemplating her.

"What do you want?" she demanded of the unseen presence.

Silence.

"What do you want!" the poor woman angrily cried.

Silence reigned for an endless count of heartbeats.

Norill waited in a perverse sense of ecstasy. Truly helpless, all she could do was wait for the fatal moment she met her destiny – when a bullet fatally impacted her lungs, head, or heart, rendering her merely what she had always been, an impermanent traveler in this world.

A deep voice spoke in German.

This was it.

Norill diligently listened to the words, but to her, they meant nothing.

In those precious seconds, she burned brightly, waiting, knowing that all she perceived of this life and any dreamt of future depended solely on the seconds to come. In that instant, she was truly limitless.

The hood jerked upward, causing her eyes to clasp shut in pain against the abrupt shift in light. The voice speaking German continued behind her as she struggled to bring her eyes quickly into focus. When they at last did, her breath seized in her chest in both disbelief and horror.

"Vinni?"

The blind woman's hood lay on the deck; disoriented, the older woman clearly was trying to reconcile both her surroundings and to ascertain whom she shared the space with.

"Norill?" she quizzically wondered. "Oh, you poor, stupid girl."

"Vinni!" Norill demanded of her friend, but the older woman said nothing more.

The hood was unexpectantly plunged back down on Norill's head, obscuring her sight. She was aware of a distinct click.

"Nnnooooo!!!!!!!!!!" she helplessly wailed even as the shot discharged.

Norill's mind recoiled as she heard both the sickening impact, last gasp, and final cruel passage of her friend's body to the cold, steel deck of the ferry.

She screamed in abject horror, in murderous rage.

The voice behind her, again spoke in German, but this time there was something different about it. A sense of unfathomable familiarity beset her.

Who spoke these cruel commands?

Before she could conceive of an answer, sounds assaulted her that made it clear that another potential victim was being summoned.

"No more! No more!" Norill sightlessly cried as she sensed someone being harshly seated across from her.

"I'm sorry," Norill wailed. "I'm so sorry. Don't kill them, don't kill them! Kill me, kill me!!!"

She could hear the bag being removed from the other's head. Again, from behind her, she heard the unmistakable sound of a round being loaded into a gun's chamber.

"No! No! Stop it! Stop it!" Norill struggled once more to stand, but she was cruelly restrained.

"It's all right, Norill," a new voice sweetly intoned, one that recognized the hopelessness of the situation.

Norill sagged helplessly against the bench as the abhorrent reality unfolded before her. She wept.

"Vinni secretly taught my husband braille to stop …."

The thought would never be finished as a bullet struck down Mrs. Erickson.

Anger swelled within Norill as a primal scream erupted from her, but still, she could not move. Her body surged again helplessly against those who restrained her.

"I'm going to kill you!"

She vowed to those manipulating her, who were responsible for these blatant atrocities.

"I'm going to KILL YOU!!!!"

Thunderous heartbeats passed before she realized that her efforts were being met with low, humorless laughter, given by those who knew she was at their complete mercy.

They were enjoying this.

It was sickening.

Norill worked to slow her breathing and calm herself. She wouldn't give them the satisfaction of being their tormented plaything. Better to die with some shred of dignity.

Her modest efforts were greeted with more knowing laughter.

Unexpectantly, she heard the retreat and shifting of booted feet. Unprompted, a new restraining, strong hand rested on her shoulder to convey that she'd not been left unattended. A potent reminder of control and the uselessness of escape.

A nearly unfathomable sense of loss gripped her heart as she thought of the cruel fates of Vinni and Mrs. Erickson.

Gone. Forever.

Was there any ember of hope left to guide her to freedom?

Norill's mind was a conflicting mosaic of contradictory emotions, but she clung to a thin, clear strand of reason as one must in a storm-tossed sea, desperately seeking salvation.

Act now!

Fighting one or two now versus an unknown number of assailants potentially on this ship was her best chance. Even if they shot her, at least she'd die trying rather than passively accepting her end. The image of her father in his smart, crisp military uniform accompanied this thought.

She smiled to herself, knowing he'd approve of her courage.

Norill frantically sank to the deck. Her elbows banged painfully onto the metal flooring with a sharp clang. Frantically, she began to crawl, hoping she could exact escape by working her way under the benches. She paused every few meters in harried attempts to remove the hood from her head. Each attempt brought her closer to succeeding.

The deck shook as her guard began to move purposefully after his charge. The hood, at last, tumbled away. Norill shifted her frenzied course accordingly. A whistling sound pinged dully nearby, but it still took her an instant to realize what was happening.

She was being shot at.

Her heart felt like it would explode, it was beating so fast.

Another ricochet struck the deck near her outstretched leg. The bullet smashed into a nearby pipe, releasing a boiling stream of steam upon her.

Norill cried out in misery as she rolled desperately away.

The full measure of the pain from her burns was just beginning to register when she was shot through the leg. Time froze. A hand gripped the back of her head.

Then she remembered nothing.

*

Norill's neck hurt. No, her head. Her side, her leg.

Each level of renewed consciousness brought a new pain and fear. Her hands were still bound but behind her and more loosely than before. As she finally opened her eyes, Norill realized she was awkwardly laid out on a bench. She gingerly attempted to shift her position as the lack of circulation in her left arm flooded her nervous system with the sensation of pins and needles poking her.

How long had she been like this?

The rumble of powerful engines throbbed steadily

through the ship. They were underway.

Her perspective on the deck pitched and heaved as flashes of lightning bathed her surroundings in alternating waves of shadow and intense light. She felt the reverberations from the thunder more than she heard them.

The wound in her leg had been wrapped, but the agony from her numerous injuries was causing her vision to pulse in sympathy to the beat of her heart. She fought against the pressing urge to vomit and her body's relentless summons to sleep.

Norill blinked in concentration as she realized she must focus to survive.

Why kill the others and save her?

She had nothing to offer other than as a source of cruel amusement. Her eyes were drawn to a crimson swath of blood moving slowly across the deck below. A vivid testament to violence.

Was that her blood? Mrs. Erickson's? Vinni's?

If she was crying, she couldn't even feel it now.

The final words of her murdered friends lodged in her mind. Vinni had acted as if the answer should be obvious, whereas, Mrs. Erickson had attempted to convey critical facts before meeting her fate.

Fate.

On some unconscious level, it made some perverse sense that this was happening to her, as if she'd always known this exact scene would be playing out this precise way, one to guide Norill to her destiny. The surreal thought was at once both reassuring and unnerving.

She felt more exposed and vulnerable than at any point in her life. A life that could be forfeit any second.

"There are three hooded figures behind you."

All Norill was conscious of was the beating of her heart as these words scarred time and cast her into stunned disbelief, every thought arrested. Still, her body moved independent of her mind.

"I can hear you struggling to turn. My advice is don't," there was only the slightest of pauses. "Don't throw their lives away. I need you to listen."

Norill wanted to speak but ceaseless anguish and stark knowledge threatened to at last break her will. She couldn't even bring herself to wonder how this was possible.

But surreal as it was, this was now her reality. A fate she could not outrun.

"Why don't you ask me in German, Rejor?" she cried.

Again, there was a pause.

"Go on. Ask me," she softly begged.

There was no response aside from the muted shifting sound of his cane upon the deck.

It hurt too badly for her to do much more than shift her weight on the bench. Her emotions surged.

"Are you going to shoot me. Shoot me again? Murder more of my friends, you unimaginable bastard? Talk to me! You fucking coward!" Norill raged as her temple inadvertently banged against the back of the bench seat. "Traitor, traitor," she whispered as the pain sharpened her mind's focus.

A tentative hand descended upon her face and traced fingers up into her hair.

"I can't blame you for your hate, Norill. There is so much I must explain. And our time is very short," her brother earnestly entreated. "You must listen. Will you listen to me?"

She made no motions and made no sounds for him to respond to as he withdrew his hand from her head. He tried again.

"Listen as we once did by that stream that runs through the pines near the southern pastures on the farm."

"I hate you," Norill finally said in a dead voice. "I hate you."

"Listen!" he barked as his hand struck the back of the

wooden bench, sending brief aftershocks down the seat.

"I'd rather you just kill me," she quietly asserted. "Like you did to Vinni … Mrs. Erickson … how many others, Rejor? How many have you sent to their deaths? Just kill me and be done with it, you senseless monster."

Seemingly from nowhere, Rejor produced a knife. Norill stiffened until his intentions became clear. Her bonds fell to the deck as again the knife vanished to be replaced by a gun.

"Sightless, sightless, remember? I'm quite sensible, dear sister," he assured her before continuing. "Do you have any idea what the Nazis do to my kind, Norill? To the handicapped, eh? They murder us. How terrifying was it when you were wearing that hood? How relieved were you when some unseen force spared your life, granted you mercy? I just did Vinni a favor compared to what they would have done."

What could she say?

She was grateful to have even a few more miserable moments of precious life and the persistent rumors of Nazi atrocities against all manner of "undesirables" by the so-called master race were all too well-known, if not witnessed firsthand.

Still, Norill shook her head.

"We both know who and what the Nazis are. Do you really think that betraying the resistance somehow protects you? That giving yourself over to the very thing we all swore to destroy, even at the cost of our very lives, makes you immune to their inhuman practice of eradicating the weak?"

She paused a measure of heartbeats. A vibrant wave fueled by both pity, anger, and anguish weighed upon her as she gazed up at her brother.

How could he have become so lost?

"You're the worst kind of traitorous fool for even having the notion of trusting them," she assured him. "They're vipers, and they will turn on you as soon as your usefulness to them ends."

Rejor laughed.

"Dear sister, given the number of Norwegian resistance cells I've already eradicated for them and have the potential to deliver, it'll be quite some time before the viper turns on me. By then, the war may be over, and no one will be the wiser as to my ultimate role in it," he smirked before placing a lone finger in front of his lips. "I have their secrets, as well as my own. The gifts of being a trusted intel officer."

"You want to humiliate them," Norill breathed. "Play one side against the other …"

"Keep each in the dark, until it's too late for them to recognize the trap, then let them struggle against the inevitable end their weaknesses have bestowed upon them. Survive," Rejor smiled as he tapped a finger against the top of the bench before pointing it toward her. "That is power. That is what will see us through to the end of this war."

"Yes. And all it costs are innocent lives," Norill said in a haunted tone. "And your soul."

Rejor shook his head.

"Don't be naïve, Norill. We all choose sides in life. This war has put blood on all our hands in one way or another. I'm simply putting myself above this war. And I'm saving you from a hopeless cause."

"By destroying everyone I love?" her heart wept.

Rejor leaned downward over her. Norill's reflection stared starkly back from the concealing sunglasses he wore.

"Time for a bit of honesty on your part. How many people did those you love help to orchestrate the deaths of, huh? How many innocent people are dead because of your efforts? Think about the logic. The Nazis will leave if we blow up that sympathizer's café. The Germans will lose hope if we strangle this officer's Norwegian lover. This intel will help another Allied bombing raid that will rid us of the Germans, while killing hundreds. The enemy hates children; and yet, we sacrifice our own during botched raids and then comfort ourselves by calling them innocent bystanders to soften the blow."

Norill felt as if the blackness of the glasses was consuming her as he continued.

"You only know a fraction of the carnage. Day after endless day as all those messages descended upon me from various cells … the true cost of this war is appalling once laid fully bare before you. You say I'm a monster? Perhaps that is what I've become, but I wonder who the real monster is when we repeatedly carry out and condone such actions against our own. Are we no less monsters for doing so? They can't all be Nazi sympathizers, can they?"

Norill withered as she considered his words and the unimaginable loss of lives.

"You were in a position to change such mistakes …," she began.

"No!" he snapped. "No, they didn't want to listen to the cripple. What could he possibly know? Censure him, cast him away. We are often not so different from them in that sense, are we? So, yes, I was obedient and ordered death after death for the resistance hoping, praying it would solve something for our country … for me. But it never did. And then I came to realize that I was just a pawn. A lamb for the slaughter, filling hours with baseless platitudes and token words of comfort for my actions. Now the dead just stare back at me in the blackness and the war continues."

He straightened.

"Then I learned of the intel regarding the weapons the Nazis are close to developing. Remarkable. Power unlike anything the world has seen. They will fundamentally change the very nature of warfare. Norway has nothing to counter such apocalyptic instruments of destruction. Why sacrifice my nation needlessly? Why wait for the final bombs to drop to be rounded up and taken off to the camps? Better to be the architect of my own fate and that of our country. In that there is hope," he nodded. "Ultimately, I'll be the savior of our nation."

Norill's heart opened to the twisted man before her. It swelled to behold one she loved who was so utterly lost.

How had she missed seeing what he'd truly become?

"Conspiring to give our country to the Germans is not hope …it's treason," Norill reached up in painful desperation and grabbed her brother's face.

A part of her only saw the boy she'd once known. In that moment, every part of her begged to save him.

"You were a good person once," she began as tears rolled freely down her face. "Surely, even you can still recognize these warped sentiments as fear driven fantasies. Rejor, oh Rejor. End this. You and I can go far away from here. Far from this war and set things right. I promise I'll find a way. I'm sorry if I haven't been there for you while you struggled alone through this. I love you, Rejor. Despite all this, I love you. You are my brother, wounded and lost though we both might be, we are a part of each other. Don't let your legacy in this world be one of hate and fear. Come back to me."

For an instant, one of his hands reached up and lovingly clasped hers. Then Rejor withdrew just enough to be able to remove his glasses, exposing his vacant eyes.

"They say other senses grow stronger when one is lost. It is a lie. I was sacrificed long ago, Norill. I know something of suffering because of unfair circumstances. Vinni never understood that. Her lessons when I was first forced to learn braille were full of sentiment and life wisdom as she understood it, but she never was willing to acknowledge that we weren't the same. She was born never knowing sight. I was. How could she possibly understand all I lost when mother made her abhorrent choice to sacrifice me? Like you, she believed I was weak. And then Lisbeth … I'm so close now to proving you both wrong. Just a few loose ends to tie up," Rejor noted as he lifted a gun into view.

"Tell me about Lisbeth," Norill prompted, hoping she could still reach some part of him. "Tell me about the box with your ring, the torn letter, that ticket. What happened to her? Tell me."

For only the second time in this insane conversation, Rejor seemed to soften. He looked down on her with a wistful expression of pity.

"You've never really been in love, have you, Norill?"

"No," she admitted immediately. "But you were. What happened?"

Rejor straightened and tapped the side of his gun against his temple as a surge of emotion passed through him before he hung his head.

"She took Lisbeth from me. Piece by piece. Tried to hide the miscarriage. The cripple doesn't deserve happiness. He's too imperfect. Such a disappointment. Can't be trusted to manage his own affairs. Well, no more."

The steel in his voice with this final pronouncement terrified Norill. He returned his attention fully to her.

"When I lost my vision, the last fading image I can recall is an arch of stars retreating upward from me, then darkness. An eternal night. Which of these three should I bring into everlasting darkness before we depart to our future?"

Norill had almost completely forgotten that lives depended on her actions.

Without thinking she swatted the gun from her brother's grasp and sent it spinning across the metal deck. Only then did her eyes turn to witness three nearby hooded figures, heads downcast. Suddenly one of them pitched violently forward as a crimson fountain projected viciously outward from their head before pooling beneath them.

"Sounds like my compatriot wasn't impressed with your efforts," Rejor cruelly noted.

Absent thought, Norill abruptly attempted to lurch off the bench in a desperate attempt to obtain the abandoned gun on the deck. Every nerve in the lower half of her body erupted at once as her wounded leg collapsed immediately.

She crumpled to the deck, wailing in unmitigated pain.

"Just as well," Rejor coldly noted. "My partner would have struck you down the moment you got anywhere near that gun. Besides, it's not even loaded."

Norill pounded the deck.

She could smell the iron rich blood beneath the unfortunate soul who'd just been summarily executed by her brother and his compatriot. Norill breathed deeply as a profound and abiding certainty fixed itself into the core of her being.

Death no longer mattered. She must stop Rejor, despite the likely outcome.

He could not be allowed to leave this ship alive.

What would she become if she killed him? Destroyed her last surviving sibling?

She divorced herself from such thoughts. They would only bring doubt to abhorrent actions that now must be embraced. Both her life and perhaps the entire Norwegian resistance depended on it.

"I thought I got to choose," she admonished. "You asked me which I'd pick. You cheated," she calmly interjected as she hauled herself back up onto the bench and off the freezing deck.

The bandage on her leg was becoming saturated with blood, and Norill slipped several times as she at last regained her seat on the bench. She would play his twisted game, if only to stall for time.

Surprisingly, this turn seemed to delight her brother.

“Very well,” Rejor agreed in manipulative amusement. “But I’ll give you a moment before we continue. I can practically hear you shivering.”

Norill was, in fact, quaking with a toxic combination of fatigue, cold, terror, blood loss, and pain. Still, her mind raced.

How could she save the two people who were left?

“Why do you want these people dead?” she countered.

Rejor recoiled a measure.

“These people,” Norill again fought to struggle upward through the pain. “Are they enemies, pawns, innocents? Victims? What are they, Rejor? You control us all. What are they to you?”

Her brother staggered back from the bench as Norill finally rose and could clearly see the two hooded figures he approached.

“All of those, they are all of those,” he tapped his cane near one of them as he fixed himself upon his surroundings.

A new thought sprinted into Norill’s mind.

Where was Rejor’s compatriot?

Her eyes darted about the entirety of the passenger cabin. As she did so, an unexpected sight summoned her attention to the aft of the ship. A single point of wildly shifting light arched outward from its sources and was tracing the path of the roiling waves as it doggedly pursued the vessel she was on through the stormy waters along the coast.

Who could be after them?

No sane person would idly be out here on a night such as this. Maybe it was Jacks making a last desperate attempt to either flee or to get aboard!

Her brother could sense her diverted attention.

“If you’re wondering where my sharpshooter is you can forget it. He’s too well-trained,” Rejor boasted.

Norill grimly laughed.

"There are only so many doors," she reminded her duplicitous brother.

Rejor took her lightheartedness in stride.

"By all means, Norill, if you want to test that notion please make some attempt to free these two before I summon them to their final destinies," her brother suggested.

She made no motion.

"No? Well. You wanted me to let you choose, so choose," he taunted.

Norill stopped considering the distant but now steadily approaching light of the other ship to examine Rejor's prisoners – a man and a woman. They were heaving muffled breaths, obviously gagged beneath bags over their heads. Both wore enough heavy clothing, including gloves, in addition to the obscuring hoods each wore, that it was all but impossible to discern clues about who these people were.

An icy sensation rose up Norill's back as she realized their anonymity made her horrific choice that much worse. But she must keep Rejor talking if she were to save any of them.

"Have your sharpshooter kill them," she bid. "It won't matter which I chose, you're certain to kill them both. There is no mercy left in you."

There was but the faintest of pauses.

"Come now. I told you one-day we'd play a game. Get into the sport of the evening, my dear sister. Gamble. I swear at least one of these people is going to die tonight," Rejor evenly stated. "Their own choices have brought them this fate, not you. You're absolved, so choose."

Norill was about to challenge him before an unexpected wave of pain shot through her leg. She glanced down in unforeseen agony. Blood was pooling and throbbing in the wounded calf she'd perched upon the bench. Knowing she must move, she agonizingly hauled herself slowly down the length of the seat, leaving a glistening smear of blood in her wake.

At last, she reached a post.

She clung to its sides so she could awkwardly stand. It was taking every last ounce of strength to remain upright. Norill was breathing hard, fighting through the agony and against the insistent urge to pass out. If she did, it was over.

Hope was over.

Norill closed her eyes and summoned clarity beyond the pain. She focused on taking deep, controlled breaths and slowly her head cleared as the pressure lessened.

"Who are you to make such proclamations?" Norill bitterly demanded.

This time the response was biting and immediate.

"Merely one who would see justice served. A nation without it is not worth saving. Wouldn't you agree?"

Norill would have answered, but she had more pressing needs as she sank awkwardly to the deck in the aisle facing the others and ripped more fabric from her clothing to try to cease the unfettered spate of bleeding. Her vision blurred as fingers wet with blood did everything they could to retie her dressing.

The sensation was nauseating.

Could she be dying?

She fought back tears and a rising panic. This couldn't be her end. It was so unfair.

She must keep talking.

"Why here, Rejor?! Why tonight, on this ship?" Norill finally managed after crudely applying her field dressing. She felt cold. "I know this is by design. Why kill them here?"

Rejor remained speechless for a time.

At last, he wordlessly touched each of the prisoners to determine for himself the identities of each before removing the hood from the male captive. When their eyes met, it was as if they were truly seeing each other for the first time.

Rejor savored their mutual shock.

"Nothing to say? Surely, you recognize your friend?" her brother prompted.

"Yes," Norill breathed in disbelief. She could bring herself to offer no more.

This was not the situation she'd anticipated, if indeed, she'd been able to grasp any of this unreality at all. She existed beyond reason, beyond thought; only the reason of violence and action remained.

Would she survive? Would any of them?

Her heart could only feel an immediate embrace of love. No more death, her mind cried.

"Remove his gag," Norill commanded her brother.

"Are you sure? He will only tell you lies," Rejor cautioned her.

Norill looked again at the helpless prisoner. How long had she feared this man?

She held his intense, dire gaze.

"If all he says are lies, what do you have to fear?" Norill questioned her brother.

She held his sightless gaze as the moment between them extended outward in time.

"Lies are no threat to you," she insisted as Rejor continued to hesitate. Clearly, he hadn't fully anticipated her reaction.

The blind man produced his knife in response and held it suggestively.

"You've been warned," he advised, before delicately cutting the gag loose on the prisoner.

"Talk before he kills you," Norill practically begged. "Why Gerntz, why?"

The man looked down as he subtly coughed before returning his attention fully to her.

"Your beauty," Gerntz offered by way of answer. "It began with your beauty, nothing more."

She closed her eyes as he continued.

"I was a German spy," he confessed in a somewhat raspy voice. "We knew about Vinni, but they wanted the rest of your resistance ring exposed. It was a simple mission, until I entered that parlor."

Norill felt, more than realized, that her hand had risen to her temple.

"Then you become a double agent?"

Gerntz met her eyes.

"Sigdis promised us that she could deliver all of you into our custody. But I had my doubts, and for other reasons I pressed for more time," Gerntz admitted.

They shared a long, reciprocal pause.

"Why didn't you turn me in? Why did you keep saving me?" Norill quietly asked.

Gerntz sighed and lowered his head again.

"You were … special to me. I didn't want to believe at first that you were capable of such actions," Gerntz nodded as he recounted his memories. "Then your brother approached me, first through a series of contacts and later in person. That's when I made my choice to become a double agent. I could get us to safety and accomplish my mission for The Reich."

"Ah, yes, *Der Reich*," Rejor sarcastically intoned. "Tell me, Gerntz, did you ever truly believe in any of it?"

"I suppose as much as you once cared for your country, Rejor," the other darkly responded. "But I have seen too much. All I want now is peace, a future far from death and war."

"Such noble sentiments," Rejor agreed. "That's what made you so easy to turn. Would you believe he's lying to you even now, Norill? Tell her the truth. I think you owe her that much."

Gerntz's eyes filled with both alarm and self-loathing.

"Tell her or I will," Rejor threatened.

Gerntz shot a look of pure loathing at his tormentor before continuing.

"My duty … I coerced your father's signature to sign his lands over to the Reich during interrogation," Gerntz sank in his seat a measure.

"You what?" Norill asked breathlessly.

She and Gerntz again stared wordlessly at one another, but this time for a much different reason.

"Our father died under this man's torture!" Rejor voice rang against the metal decking.

Again no one spoke, only the storm outside and steady thrum of the engines plying them through the deluge dared to intrude upon the moment.

"How do you know this?" Norill finally questioned.

"Do you think I couldn't find out such information …," her brother angrily began before being cut off.

"He didn't have to find out. I told him," Gerntz vehemently protested. "Your father wanted me to tell you about his fate. And I was lying. I didn't become a double agent here, I already was one when I arrived," he confessed.

Norill could only feel the pain inside, the doubts, the questions. Some twisted part of her wanted the sharpshooter to end this, but her fortitude was far stronger.

The spy resumed.

"Your father was part of a special Allied infiltration unit that was working to sabotage the German weapons program here in Norway. By the time I arrived in country, he'd already been captured. I managed to get myself assigned to the detention center where the few surviving members of his unit were being held. There, I was able to convince him of my connection to the Allies. But I also had a role to play if I was to remain above suspicion. We both knew time was short."

Here Gerntz paused, making sure he had Norill's full attention before continuing.

"He was convinced that the resistance was in danger. He wanted me to continue my dual role as a spy for both sides as a cover and to root out the corruption that had led to his team's end, to save his family. In exchange, he would give me information on how to help slow German weapons development. In a matter of weeks, I was able to use it to assassinate several key players in these specialized programs. After, they were forced to move certain aspects of the programs into the countryside, small towns where no one would look. That and your father's last wishes brought me here. He only signed the papers to turn your family farm over to the Reich after my efforts to impact the weapons development proved successful. It was he who sent me to Rejor. And so, I trusted your brother. Then tonight happened."

There was a blatant accusation in the statement. Could Gerntz possibly think that she was involved with Rejor's plans?

"The ambush? We were horrified by what we saw," Norill openly attested.

Gerntz studied her face.

His very life depended on his reading of this woman's character. Her gaze became one with his and did not break.

There was now a truth between them.

"It would seem your brother played us both," he finally said. "So many needlessly led to the slaughter by me. Use an enemy to destroy an enemy. There have been signs, ones I chose to ignore, thinking I was pursuing my mission without obstruction. But Rejor's orders for me become more erratic, more open to question. If only I'd had the courage to do so. But I got caught in the web, same as you."

Norill's pained face could not look away from him, their

own mistakes were embodied in the other. Perhaps, if they'd ever been able to trust each other, none of this would now be happening.

The other man finally stirred.

"Yes, too bad, Gerntz. I may have been the architect, but you've been the public face of my efforts. It is you who will be blamed for all that has occurred. And thanks to your efforts, I have an unexpected bonus. Norill, please note the detonator cables running along the sides and ceiling of the cabin," Rejor instructed.

Now drawn to them, her eyes perceived more and more of the innocuous looking wires crossing all over the ship's interior.

"There's a shipment of German heavy water[6], a key element to this new weapon onboard this ship that was stolen by the Allied commando team that was slaughtered tonight. It was to be destroyed out here after we boarded a second ship, but I see no reason to send such an invaluable commodity to the bottom of the sea. Such material should be offered to the highest bidder. Don't you agree?" her brother prompted.

"And what? You keep me alive to help you with this insane plan?" Norill asked in revulsion. "To watch you profit off the deaths and betrayals of patriots and loved ones?"

Her brother grew annoyed.

"I keep you alive because we're family. Because you've been the only member of that family who always listened. We can build a better world, Norill. That's what we all fight for. The war no longer controls us, but we it," Rejor insisted. "Join me!"

Norill attempted to move, but her awkward efforts brought only one result. The searing pain was crippling when it struck her with its full force. Instead of rising, she sank mercifully closer to the deck, as she drew short breaths

6 A key component in the Nazi quest to create a nuclear weapon.

through the agony.

"Is that why you had to get rid of Vinni? Mr. Erickson … his wife? All those soldiers you had murdered tonight. Is that why?" Norill cried.

Rejor moved closer to her but not so close she could touch him.

"I could tell you they're responsible for their own ends, but I doubt that's the answer you want," he quietly observed. "Vinni never really liked me, and I can't say I regret what happened to her tonight. We viewed our handicap completely differently; our relationship was always fraught with conflict. That continued once the war began. We disagreed on how the resistance should wage its war of attrition, but I rose through the ranks faster. I know she resented and feared the scope of my power and influence. That's why she secretly trained Erickson and his wife to read braille."

Here he paused as he again perceived Norill's efforts to regain her feet.

What good could she possibly hope such a struggle would do?

Still there must be a reason she kept trying.

As he listened, he pictured her as a young girl, the image of her he'd long since fixed in his mind's eye since losing his sight. Maybe all she wanted was a measure of dignity or was too cold on the deck … or the purpose behind her attempts could represent some threat of which he was unaware.

"My sharpshooter, Norill. Don't forget my sharpshooter," he cautioned.

He was able to control his voice, but inwardly Rejor's sense of unease was growing. He'd expected a more dramatic notice from his compatriot in response to his reminder to Norill.

Why did they remain silent?

To make matters worse, the storm and seas were becoming more violent, forcing Rejor to divide his attention as he struggled to maintain his balance. Her lack of response was unnerving.

He listened carefully.

What was she doing?

If only the clergyman hadn't been arrested, he'd have another set of eyes to use. Alas, thought Rejor, such men served their uses in war and subterfuge, but were ultimately too wedded to mortality to not be overwhelmed by the true nature of the world.

Fool. It mattered little which side had finally betrayed the man. It was the only outcome that could ever be for one who attempted to appease both sides in the name of peace.

Rejor tried to picture his surroundings.

She couldn't be reckless enough to think pulling any of the detonation wires would seriously disrupt his plans. Certainly, she wasn't trying to reach the prisoners in a vain attempt to free them?

What if she was laying a trap for him once he moved?

He immediately dropped to the deck and began to feel around until his fingertips found what they sought. Blood. Whatever she was doing, she was leaving a trail.

Rejor smiled. A hunter on the prowl.

"Erickson was Vinni's little pet project. A spy with one purpose, to spy on me. I must assume he or his wife read every piece of information you passed on after you dropped the messages down that old laundry chute to the basement of the bookstore. Rather clever actually," he noted as he chose a direction of Norill's bloody trail to follow.

"If she attempts to free the prisoners or attack me, you'll have to shoot her," Rejor suddenly cried out to his unseen comrade.

The directive was unnecessary, the words were meant for Norill's benefit.

Again, he became reticent and poured all his concentration into probing his surroundings; still he could not divine where exactly she was or what she was trying to do. Rejor must keep her distracted.

"Once I discovered Vinni's little game, I realized they, like all the others, could be useful to me. As my operations grew increasingly sophisticated, it became easier to turn resistance cells against one another, foster fear and confusion, and to turn allies upon each other. Erickson's death certainly accomplished all of those things for me," he crowed. "You're going to be so surprised when you learn who carried that out."

A sudden, familiar sound attracted his attention seconds before a harsh metallic ping near his left hand caught Rejor completely unprepared. He reared back and froze on the deck.

"You were never a good liar," Norill's voice admonished, sounding at once near and far from him. "Call off your sharpshooter."

Rejor's honed mind quickly deduced the basics. He shook his head.

"I knew you didn't believe me that my gun was unloaded," he wryly stated as he recognized the significance of the sound moments before. "I'm guessing you've found somewhere with just enough cover to make a shot difficult and that you have my gun trained on me. Five shots left. Even if you use one of them on me, you can't save the prisoners or yourself. My sharpshooter will never let any of you off this ship alive."

"Who's the other prisoner, Gerntz?" Norill demanded, ignoring her brother's grim assessment.

"I don't know," the spy admitted.

"Can you free yourself?" Norill asked.

"No," Gerntz quickly replied.

"I'm perfectly willing to let her tell her story if you stop this nonsense, Norill," Rejor volunteered. "You're sure to find it interesting. Or I could just have her executed now, like the others. They're really only still alive for your benefit and to keep me entertained before the rendezvous."

There was no response.

"Shall I end the game?" Rejor offered.

Norill cursed but said no more as a relative silence again fell over them. The weight of the gun in her sweaty, blood-encrusted hands shifted.

What would happen if she pulled the trigger?

The burning image of a fatal bullet breaking her brother's body tore through her thoughts. In that instant a part of her wanted to throw the gun away.

How could the grim realities of this world have fixed upon her heart and mind such a repulsive idea?

But the fact of what Rejor had become left her bereft of any real options.

He must die.

Whatever happened beyond the moments to come, she must ensure he never left this ship alive. A seemingly endless march of time passed.

"Call off your sharpshooter. I'm coming out," she finally bid.

"Let's not be careless, Norill. The gun first. Slide it to me across the deck," Rejor commanded.

He heard it before the object impacted against his right shoe. He retrieved it, and after a quick examination, tossed it behind him resulting in a series of clangs that seemed to echo his annoyance.

It was all but useless without the bullets she'd liberated from it. He could have pressed the matter further, but time was becoming an issue.

Still, he wanted her to understand. Needed her to understand. Even if afterward, he was compelled to kill her.

"We keep our word, let her come out and approach the others," Rejor loudly ordered as he rose from the deck and reassessed his bearings. "Come on, Norill. You won't be harmed, I promise."

Cautiously, his sister stirred, both for fear of the still unseen sharpshooter and the incessant agony from her wound.

She was weak.

It had taken a tremendous amount of exertion to seek this shelter, even though it had proven to be only a temporary one. The passage to the prisoners was daunting, one that forced her to crawl most of the way. By the end of her journey, the entirety of her being felt saturated in sweat and blood.

She awkwardly took up a seat on the bench at a right angle from the prisoners, with Rejor standing between them.

"Patience Gerntz," he advised. "I can practically hear you grinding your teeth."

"I swear you'll die before I do," the other man vowed. "And I'll be sure to repay every cruelty you've visited on innocents tenfold when I do."

Rejor laughed, before his stoic mask resumed.

"An amusing thought from one in your position. Something for one of us to look forward to I suppose. Empty threats aside, I do have a promise to keep to my sister."

"Norill, he's toying with you," Gerntz urgently advised.

She barely reacted as she continued to heave deep breaths and fought the urge to give into her unrelenting exhaustion. Of course, Rejor was toying with them, but the longer he talked, the more time it gave that pursuing ship to intercept them. In that lay her last, best hope for salvation. Her only hope.

Hurry up Jacks, she willed.

Could she free the prisoners?

Her exhausted mind attempted to ponder the impossible as she began to closely analyze the hooded, female prisoner.

Norill focused on every minute detail until her heart seized in her chest as a slow, abhorrent, impossible suspicion began to dawn.

Her lips unconsciously parted wanting to release a scream, but the unrelenting cascade of emotion inside her stifled the impulse. Every essence of her being fought to be elsewhere. She wanted to be anyplace else but living through what was about to come.

Her anguished eyes turned to Gerntz.

"Do you believe in fate?" she softly asked him as a tear graced her dirty cheek.

"Fate?" he quizzically returned, having witnessed with alarm the twisting processing of emotions that was playing out across Norill's face.

Emotion was making it hard for her to speak.

"Fate," Norill whispered, for the longer she studied the woman, the more horrifying the reality about to unfold became. "That our choices did not bring us here in this moment, that all of this has forever been destined to be. I used to think my father was crazy when he'd talk of fate, how it shapes us and controls our lives. But right now, fate is the only answer I can possibly embrace. If my choices, my mistakes brought us all to this then I am truly lost. Truly sorry."

Norill urgently turned her attention to her brother.

"Don't do this, Rejor," she begged. "Please, if you've ever loved me, please don't do this."

Rejor lowered his head in acknowledgement to the raw emotion in his sister's voice. Then he again drew this knife and began to stalk toward the prisoners opposite Norill.

He turned on her.

"Fate, it figures Father would fill your head with such nonsense. It's not fate, it's about the choices we make!" Rejor intensely declared as he grabbed the top of the hood on the woman's head. "We are marked by our choices. By the violence of reason. And it is only time that hides who we truly are."

The concealing hood was removed.

This time Norill did scream as all her worst fears stared helplessly back at her. Or rather, one eye stared back at her, the other was now gone from her gagged mother's blood-stained face.

Mother and daughter shared excruciating tears as Norill voicelessly mouthed, "I love you," to the woman on the opposite bench.

"Not quite the face you remember, I suppose," Rejor coldly observed.

Norill ignored him, seeking any type of insight she could perceive from her mother.

The older woman's remaining eye franticly locked on hers before flicking downward repeatedly to the deck. Her child glanced quickly to the nearby discarded gun that Rejor had cast aside once he'd discovered the bullets had been removed. She locked eyes with her mother as the negligible weight of the bullets she'd dumped into her coat pocket suddenly became as heavy as lead weights.

The message was clear.

If by some miracle she could obtain the gun, she could end this, assuming the sharpshooter did not act first. She needed a diversion, but what could possibly obfuscate her actions?

"An eye for an eye," Norill finally, grimly acknowledged to her brother. "Jesus, Rejor."

"One for you, one representing me," Rejor gloated as he gestured with his knife.

"I wish you could see it," Norill harshly said. "See what you've done to her."

"Ah, dear sister, I wish I could," he chillingly rejoined.

A slow smile spread sickeningly across his face. Her rage rose.

"Don't absolve her before she can defend herself," he thundered. "Afterall, I wouldn't be the man I am today without her. Blind. Crippled. Hobbled by undesirable traits. You asked me earlier about Lisbeth. Mother's an expert on relationships. Decided my wife's issues with me were enough to end my marriage without discussion. Urged her to leave me, even before Lisbeth lost our baby. Then she did. Mother was even kind enough to pass along Lisbeth's note to me explaining why she left me, with a ticket so we could get counseling together. Be grateful you never fell in love, Norill. Mother could have only ever have ruined it for you. Treated you like a child because you weren't perfect."

"Then Lisbeth's alive?" Norill wondered.

"It doesn't matter," Rejor bitterly declared. "She died to me when she betrayed me by leaving."

A tense silence descended upon them.

"What do you expect me to say, Rejor?" Norill indignantly challenged. "You mutilated our mother, and for what? To prove you could, to satisfy some twisted need for vengeance …."

"Nothing so petty," Rejor quickly responded in harsh tones. "Her crimes extend well beyond our shared history."

"What do you mean? Her work with the resistance …?"

This time the words died on her lips as she beheld her brother's expression.

"You called me a monster; yet you never question her actions," he accused, taking a step closer to his mother.

Norill's muscled tensed.

"You judge me. If you wish to survive, if you wish to learn truth, judge her now," Rejor instructed as he sliced quickly through his mother's gag.

Norill's mother practically spat the offending piece of cloth away from her mouth as an expression of burning hatred set in stone upon her countenance as she fixed her remaining eye upon her murderous son. She coughed as the lusty gasps of air she'd in taken stung her suddenly overwhelmed lungs.

The storm outside was becoming more violent as the deck unexpectantly shifted several times before resuming a more even keel. Norill did not fail to notice the calculating look Gerntz cast toward her brother when this happened. She knew he must be scheming some sort of action against their captors. In order to give him time, she must keep Rejor focused on their mother.

"Are you all right?" Norill asked the older woman.

Her mother released an anguished laugh.

"He intends to kill us both," she advised. "His hatred knows no bounds, Norill. I can live with the fact that I'm facing my end, but not that I've failed so completely as a mother."

Norill could see that her strategy was both one-part confession, the other, distraction. Rejor's reaction was almost instantaneous.

"You failed at that ages ago, Mother. Stop attempting to manipulate your daughter as well. Tell her, tell her of your crimes," her son tersely demanded.

Norill held her mother's eye.

She wanted to see reassurance there, that Rejor's statements and accusations were nothing but the ravings of a delusional mind. But as she gazed into that sole, remaining eye, Norill knew her mother was repressing something immensely painful. So much so that she had to look away and new tears began to accumulate.

"What? What is it, Mother?" Norill paused as the agonized expression on her mother's face crumbled into abject misery.

"Tell her," Rejor ordered as he loomed menacingly over his mother with the still drawn knife.

The deck heaved again and it took more than a few minutes of relative peace before those assembled could again return their full attention to the drama unfolding before them.

"I … I…," her mother began before emotion choked off her voice.

"What?" Norill softly asked despite her profound apprehension.

Her mother's expression frightened her. The lid of the older woman's eye closed as she fought a private battle within.

"I sent your father to his death," she confessed at last in a hollow, barely recognizable voice.

"No. No. He was a soldier …," Norill immediately began to counter, but the words faltered with the shake of her mother's head.

"He was a soldier," she agreed as she lowered her head. "I took advantage of that fact and sealed his fate by sending his strike team where I did on their final mission. I had to. If there was any chance to stop the Nazis, I had to."

After a brief pause, the older woman's gaze suddenly rose. A new determination visible on the marred face.

"I am the head of the Norwegian resistance for this entire section of the country. The fourth highest placed in the nation. Not even your brother knew that until this very moment."

Norill's mother studied the stunned faces of both her children.

The deck again pitched in the heavy seas forcing everyone to clasp whatever was nearest to them for balance. The gun on the deck shifted closer to Norill.

"You're lying!" Rejor spat as he clutched a nearby pole. "This is just a trick to save your miserable life."

"How?" Norill, ever thoughtful, asked as she regained a measure of balance. "How could you, the wife of a common soldier, a farmer, have risen to that rank?"

Their mother waited, making sure she had the undivided

attention of those present.

"Because when this war began, I'd already risen to this rank. Your father and I met through our work with Norwegian Intelligence well before this war. We saw the path that the Continent was on and secretly began to take steps to set up the roots of a resistance network with those we knew we could trust long before any invasion might take place. Because we did, the Nazis efforts to control this country and develop new weapons has been hindered."

"The Allies are losing this war," Rejor ardently countered. "All you've done is postpone the inevitable ..."

"Shut up," Norill ordered, cutting him off.

Was this true? She needed to know if this was true. The answer came.

"All codes have a cypher," she began. "Mother, if you are what you claim, you should know the root of the cypher system I was taught to use."

Her mother hesitated, looking to Rejor, who'd moved a few paces back from her, closer to an entryway. Norill could tell she was struggling to accurately gauge his distance, without the depth perception she'd been able to rely on for her entire life. The younger woman's heart swelled with helplessness and pity.

Still, her daughter needed to know the truth.

"We're going to die on this ship," Norill intensely insisted, returning her mother's attention fully to her. "If you know the cypher, prove it now."

The older woman carefully considered her actions before taking them.

At first, her movement was almost imperceptible as she inched forward on the bench until she was perched on the edge. As the ship shook in the roiling waves, she did nothing to resist and allowed gravity's pull to propel her forward to the deck, landing roughly upon some of the bloody trail Norill had left.

There, she awkwardly stretched out the forefinger on her right hand and soundlessly traced the answer to Norill's demand. It remained there only long enough for her daughter to see before she rolled to erase it from existence.

"What's happening?" Rejor demanded as he began to stalk forward, knife drawn in one hand, the other thrusting downward in search of the whereabouts of his prisoner.

"Your father came to suspect you," his mother cried out to her son as he grew nearer.

This outburst temporarily arrested his efforts.

"Tell me," he darkly intoned.

"Vinni suspected you, but I wasn't convinced. I wanted you to prove me wrong. If I'm guilty of a crime, then that is it. I refused to believe that you were capable of such blind hatred, of such disloyalty. I argued that you should be allowed to clear yourself of such accusations, that your actions would reveal the truth, so I kept you in place," she admitted as he bent down and forcibly seized her with his free hand.

Norill's nerves could take no more.

"Why did Erickson die? Who killed him?" Norill grimly demanded, in part, to distract her brother, who now menacingly clutched their mother closer to him and his blade.

The ship pitched again in the waves.

The gun on the deck was almost within arm's reach now, if Norill could only lean down without being shot by the sniper. She restrained from focusing on the coveted object. Rejor might not see her interest, but if his compatriot surmised her curiosity, it might as well not exist.

She kept her attention locked on her resolute family members.

"Who ransacked the bookstore?" Norill asked as the others remained mute regarding her first two questions.

Her mother's chest heaved as a rage welled up inside her before being given voice.

"Your sister's right, I did raise a monster," the older woman blatantly told her son. "That's the real reason your wife left you. Why you'll never be a great man like your father!"

A look of pure loathing passed between them.

"Fortunately, I'm not the only monster in this family," he rejoined. "Are you mad that the Ericksons are dead or that you were beaten to the punch?"

He didn't wait for his mother to respond.

"Explain to her …," the blade of his knife drew closer to his terrified prisoner.

"Rejor, stop it!! Stop it!!!" Norill screamed.

"Erickson knew too much," Gerntz suddenly interjected.

Everyone paused to look at him. The spy sat up a bit straighter in his seat as his reasoning coalesced into what he could only rationalize as the truth.

"That's it, isn't it? He knew your mother wasn't willing to take action to remove your brother, knew that Rejor was duplicitous because he could read the braille encoded intercepts you'd deposit down the chute in the bookshop. It's the only thing that makes sense. Tell me I'm wrong," Gerntz challenged the hushed members of the cabin.

"And no, I didn't kill him if that's what you're thinking," he asserted to the unspoken question written on Norill's face.

Again, no one spoke as Gerntz words remained for uncomfortable consideration among them.

"Yes, he was a threat," Norill's mother finally confessed. "He knew I was endangering the resistance. I came to learn that Vinni had taught his wife sign language and braille years earlier. Apparently, when he grew suspicious of Rejor, he first had her translate a few of the communiqués he retrieved from the bookstore cellar before having her teach him braille as well so they could act more quickly."

"How did you learn this?" Norill asked.

Her mother looked away before responding.

"Tekla. Tekla was in training to become my replacement."

"Why her?" Norill inquired. "Why, Mother?"

The older woman hesitated, but Rejor's renewed reminder of the presence of his blade compelled her to reluctantly continue. He seemed as eager as Norill to hear these revelations.

"I guess it won't matter much now," their mother admitted. "All those who could be harmed by this are dead."

This sobering pronouncement elicited a fresh wave of sorrow within Norill. So, this madness had claimed another person dear to her heart.

Tekla was dead.

"Her father was another long-standing member of Norwegian Intelligence, one we knew and trusted fully as we took early steps to form what became the resistance. As an asset, she was ideal. She knew what her parents were and, therefore, who I was. Her natural demeanor made her at once likeable, forgettable, and most importantly, above suspicion. Erickson took her in never suspecting that part of her job was to keep an eye on him. He even tried to recruit her for the resistance," she smiled at the memory. "If only he'd known …"

"What happened to her?" Rejor demanded. "I know about her parent's deaths in the fire but …"

Her mother's eye flashed vibrantly.

"I'm afraid that after Norill disappeared, she was taken in for questioning. My operatives tell me the Nazis' summarily executed her."

Norill hung her head as the full weight of these words sank what remained of her spirit. Her body shifted unconsciously as the tempest outside again made its presence known. She must keep them talking, despite everything that was happening, she must keep them talking.

"Who killed Erickson?" her dead voice repeated.

"I did," a familiar voice from the entryway calmly asserted.

No!

Norill's eyes rose in disbelief as the unfathomable happened.

Jacks calmly entered the room with a sniper rifle in hand, trained menacingly on the prisoners. Norill's heart was in her throat, each pulse pounded in her ears as all hope died and time stopped.

"Jacks?" her voice choked and cracked.

The sight of her once would-be savior, the knowledge that it was he who had murdered her friends, that it was his cruelty and deceit that had so viciously wounded her leg, was too much to bear.

"I trusted you. I'm going to kill you," she quietly whispered. "Somehow, I'm going to kill you."

The man maliciously smirked dismissively to her remarks as he turned his attention to Rejor.

"Afraid our dear ferry captain tried to turn himself into a hero before he met his untimely end. We're adrift," Jacks informed his partner as he relaxed the barrel of the sniper rifle a bit.

Rejor cursed.

Well, that at least explained Jacks' prolonged absence in firing any shots.

"I don't suppose you know how to pilot this ship?" the blind man demanded of the soldier who simply shook his head in the negative before remembering that he needed to speak.

"No."

"I could do it," Gerntz offered seconds later.

"Why, Jacks? Why?" Norill softly asked as she leaned back fully in utter exhaustion on the bench.

A double image of the man flooded her vision as he approached her. How much blood had she lost?

He leaned down to study first her face, then her makeshift tourniquet above her wound.

"Does it matter?" he replied as he tightened the wrapping.

A wave of pain coursed the length of her body.

"It does to me," she finally answered after it subsided, and her vision began to clear.

"It's my job," he evenly explained.

"I work for German counter-intelligence. I was placed in England well before the war started. My mission coming here was twofold: make sure the Allied mission to destroy our experimental weapons program failed and to test how loyal to the Reich our friend Gerntz was. Both have proven successful. Before we left Britain, I'd already passed on our planned flight path and target information, so our fighters were ready to intercept us upon our arrival over Norway."

"But you could have died," Norill dumbfoundedly said.

Jacks shrugged.

"A possibility, but when you've faced death as often as I have, such considerations become secondary," he noted. "Those Allied soldiers who survived the crashes thought they were causing disruptions as they awaited rescue, but all they've been doing is exposing more and more of the Norwegian resistance network. And now, with your mere presence, you've provided me with the most useful discovery yet. Your mother will indeed be an invaluable asset to our war effort."

He smiled as if he'd just told a particularly amusing joke at a dinner party, one completely lost on his captive audience.

"Why did you kill Erickson?" Norill persisted.

Jacks grinned.

"Insurance. To sow confusion on both sides. Same reason I ransacked the bookstore. I even arranged your release and Gerntz's purported escape all to keep you turning on each other, leaving me free to act and gather intelligence. And I must say, you've provided more than I'd ever hoped for …"

This final thought was interrupted as Norill attempted to strike the man's windpipe, but his reactions were too fast. His iron grip shattered her hand before he released it. She cried out in pain as she sprawled out, face down on the bench.

Jacks seemed completely indifferent as he stared down at her.

"None of this was personal, Norill. Behave yourself and when our U-boat arrives to take us and the cargo off, I'll try to keep them from tossing you overboard. It's the least I can do after all the help you and your family have provided me. Just a few loose ends to tie up," he proclaimed, walking away.

Her breath heaved in her lungs, but her eyes focused solely on the gun now directly before her on the deck. All she need do was stretch out her arm and her fingers could easily prize the tempting object.

But how could she hope to load the bullets in her pocket in time?

"There's no need for us to transfer to a U-boat," Rejor declared to his anxious partner.

At first, Jacks said nothing as he studied the view outside the nearby port window.

"The captain rather ably crippled the controls, Rejor. Not to mention we now have a number of bodies and precious cargo on this ship, which is quite slow even without this blasted storm. No, I'm afraid your little profiteering venture with Nazi weapons components is not to be."

"How very sad for you, dear brother," Norill grinned from the bench.

"You promised me …!" Rejor began.

"I lied!" Jacks instantly returned as he rounded back toward those assembled in the cabin before focusing solely on Rejor.

"You've proven useful to the Reich and I'll ensure that you aren't sent off to a camp for your defects, but you're far too great a liability to leave behind in Norway. Your treachery has reached its limit. You've chosen your side. Best you make peace with that now."

Then Jacks fixed his judgmental scrutiny on the most taciturn member of the cabin.

"Herr Gerntz. You've proved something of a disappointment to me. I thought you held great promise when I left Germany, but your mixed loyalties have proven your undoing. Did you seriously think that you could avoid our notice?"

Gerntz minutely shifted.

"If you had so little faith in my abilities, why did you send me into the field?" he countered.

Jacks gaze turned downward a moment before staring harshly into his underlings' eyes.

"I'd hoped my suspicious about you would be proven wrong, but there were too many signs to ignore your transient allegiance to the Fatherland. But, to answer your question, even traitors can prove useful tools. I kept waiting for you to betray me to others, why didn't you?"

Gerntz hesitated before answering, his focus briefly setting upon Norill.

"I wish I had, but then you could have exposed me. After a time, I knew you must be using me for some greater mission but by then I was in too deep," he confessed.

"I can see why you were attracted to Ms. Haugen. She is quite charming," Jacks smiled at Norill who averted her eyes at the memory of the closeness of their bodies in the woods, the false hope and feelings he'd elicited in her.

She shuddered as a new wave of pain coursed through her as the vessel again pitched aimlessly amid the increasingly furious winds, rains, and waves outside. Norill suddenly became sick upon the deck.

"We'll need help moving those barrels," Rejor noted to Jacks who nodded in stoic agreement.

"Well, Gerntz, it looks like your service to the Fatherland is not quite done. I promise to be a clean shot when it is," Jacks offered.

"First, I have one thing to take care of," Rejor dully stated. "But I'll need your help, Jacks."

"What?" his partner asked.

Rejor raised his knife over his mother's face.

"Her remaining eye must be taken," he coldly declared.

"No," Norill's hoarse voice croaked in anguish.

Jacks dispassionately considered the situation.

"She's an intel resource. I can't see how crippling her further will benefit us if we need her to review codes or documents," he coolly asserted.

Rejor drew the knife to his mother's throat.

"What if she's not alive to read anything?" he threatened.

At this, Jacks drew his rifle upward and settled into a firing position.

"And what if I just kill you here?" he challenged.

Rejor was not deterred.

"The most subtle shift of this ship will deny you of your prize," he pointed out. "The worst I can do is maim her. So, lose your prize or help me."

Jacks was obviously displeased with Rejor but couldn't see a way to guarantee a clean shot to take out his odious companion.

Clearly a new tactic was needed.

"I'm going to free Gerntz," he announced to Rejor after a moment. "He will aid you in your task."

Without waiting for any protests, Jacks withdrew a knife from his belt, and in seconds, sliced the bonds that held Gerntz, who stared in disbelief as the ropes fell to the deck. He waited for some sign that Jacks wasn't serious, but the other man just thrust his head toward the others by way of ordering Gerntz to join to them. If completing his mission successfully required the loss of this woman's other eye, so be it.

Just as Gerntz stood the lights of the ship all went out at once.

A curious, terrifying mixture of sounds that spoke of struggle, pain, and death assaulted the cabin, along with the strobing effect of lightning flashes now playing out with abandon across the whole of the blackened ship.

It took Norill what felt like an absurd amount of time to locate the gun on the deck in the darkness. Her hand repeatedly smacked clumsily downward, only to touch more flat metal, until, at last, the object she sought impacted her numbing fingers.

She lunged downward to the deck for it, landing with an unceremonious thud. Norill did her best to ignore the shooting pains in her arms as she frantically thrust a hand into her pocket, seeking the bullets there.

Fumbling fingers withdrew a mass of these, which scattered and clattered upon the shifting deck. The sounds of struggle around her grew more pronounced and desperate; and yet, she couldn't seem to get the bullets loaded into the chamber.

Finally, one snapped cleanly into place.

As she took aim at two of the struggling forms illuminated against the blackness by the lightning, a shadowy figure from the cabin's entry fired several shots in the same direction. In confusion and terror, Norill closed her eyes, felt her aim shift, before she tensed at the sensation of recoil as the gun accidently fired.

She dropped the offending weapon immediately as a light source shone directly into her eyes seconds before it raced toward her.

"Good God, Norill!" Tekla's voice intoned.

All Norill could do was raise her hands defenselessly to her face as she fought back tears as her friend hastily examined her.

"We've got to get you off this ship," Tekla declared. "It's going to blow in five minutes."

"The others?" Norill cried out. "Mother?!"

Tekla shone her light in the direction the sounds of struggle had come from.

Jacks was dead. His own knife now stuck prominently from his throat, his eyes staring vacantly forward to a future they would never behold.

Gerntz lay over his lap.

Tekla moved to examine him. It was clear from her motions that he was already dead but still she made an effort to check.

Her light then turned momentarily to Norill's mother. All Tekla did was remove her jacket and cover the older woman's face.

Near her body, fighting for air was Rejor. A gaping wound now graced his abdomen where Norill's wild bullet had settled.

His sightless eyes darted wildly.

"Don't leave me," he begged first of Tekla, then blindly toward his sister. "Don't leave me here to die alone, Norill."

Tekla trained her gun on him a moment before lowering it.

"Far better than what you deserve," she decided. "I'll grant you the mercy of meeting your end on this ship as the Lord intended."

Without a second's hesitation she turned away, leaving him to cry out repeatedly from the darkness.

"Tekla. Norill. Norill! Please Norill! Please! Take me with you! Norill! Norill!"

Neither woman spoke a word, as Tekla aided Norill's

painful journey from that macabre cabin down to the loading level of the ferry. There a smaller ship pitched wildly nearby, waiting for them.

A lone figure stood a treacherous watch near the moorings, weathering all the storm could bear upon him. As Norill grew closer, something in the man's stance suddenly flooded her with recognition.

"Haktor!" she shouted in relief and fell against his huge, soaked form.

The man offered a hasty, reassuring pat as he ushered the women toward the nearby jostling ship.

"Two minutes!" he yelled over the tempest. "Watch the rail. It's like holding a stick of butter."

Slowly, painfully, the three managed to disembark from the ferry. Seconds later, Haktor was cutting the moorings loose and waving madly to the pilot's house. The form inside wasted no time in slamming the engines to full capacity and veering urgently away from the doomed ferry.

Norill hunched down on the rain drenched deck, her eyes fixed behind the receding ship. Some part of her still longed to see Rejor attempt to save himself while the rest of her inaudibly counted the seconds.

Shortly before the end came, she dimly perceived another shape near the ferry.

It took her exhausted mind an eternity to process what she was seeing – a U-boat's conning tower now rode astride the other ship. She could see the outline of men set against the flickering lightening and unyielding waves as they moved aboard the ferry.

Norill was forced to look away when the explosion came.

The fireball was so massive, it easily consumed the visible part of the U-boat and all the men on its deck. There would be no pursuit by the enemy. As far as the Nazis would ever know, all the souls that boarded the ferry were now lost to the depths.

Strong hands gipped her, and Norill was mercifully ushered into the pilot house of the small fishing vessel. Haktor gently set her down on a pile of dry clothes and blankets that had been placed on the wooden deck. He leaned over her.

Norill studied the familiar face floating above her, a sudden thought returning to her mind.

"How old are you?" she dully asked.

"What? I'm 47. Why?"

Norill said nothing, only offering a slight nod of appreciation as her thoughts returned to their dear, dead friend. So, Vinni had won their final bet.

"Told you I'd get you out," Haktor smiled and squeezed her hand before exiting back outside.

Tekla hovered over her now, repeatedly offering water, and applying new dressings to her wounded leg. At some point in the process, Norill passed out and remained so for several hours.

*

When she awoke, it was still mostly dark, but they were clear of the storm. Tekla had not moved from her side. She smiled weakly at her friend, who fervently held Norill's hand.

"I thought you were dead," Norill breathed. "Where are we?"

"Off the Scottish coast by now," Tekla motioned her head toward the light creeping through a nearby window.

"If it hadn't been for your mother and Gerntz, you would be dead. He let us know the Nazis' plans to intercept you, but we were too late to stop the initial ambush. He also told us about Jacks, Rejor, the weaponized heavy water on the ferry. He died a hero," Tekla shook her head. "If only there'd been more time before I shot, and the deck shifted."

"I think he would have liked hearing you call him that," Norill said softly. "A hero. I think in his truest of hearts that's all he ever wanted to be."

She paused.

"Mother?"

Tekla wiped tears from her eyes but found herself unable to speak for several minutes.

"Until the day I die, she will remain the greatest person I ever have known. Without her efforts the resistance would not exist, Rejor's duplicity would not have been uncovered, and countless more lives would have been lost. I suppose she told you she ran the resistance locally?"

Norill mournfully nodded.

"She was covering for me, for you see. I trained her to be my replacement should I ever be killed. We were both to lie if ever captured to ensure the continued existence of the resistance. Regardless of her role, she was my friend … and I shall miss her and honor her memory all my days to come."

The two women held each other in shared grief for a time.

"Why me?" Norill finally asked.

Tekla was quiet as she considered the question.

"Fate," she responded at last. "And I knew no matter what, your heart will always be true."

The women embraced.

"Were you actually arrested after I vanished?" Norill asked her friend as they withdrew from each other.

"Yes, and I would have died there too if not for one of my most valuable assets rescuing me," Tekla stated as she rose from the deck and helped Norill stand upright.

The morning sunlight they now stood in was brilliant and at first it blinded Norill to the figure who helmed the small ship.

"Like you, she's lost and sacrificed much to get us all here," Tekla soberly said. "When we reach Scotland, we'll all begin again, and if you're willing, continue the fight to free our great nation.

Norill only dimly registered her friend's final words.

All she could do was stare at the sight of Sigdis at the ship's wheel, as she guided them all through the endless waves to a new life and freedom.

If you enjoyed this book please post a review online at a location of your choice to help others find them, and take a moment to recommend it to your local library